of those unfathomable places where we imagine we'll become bolder, truer versions of ourselves. This is a beautifully written and hearteningly unsentimental debut."

—Jim Shepard, author of *Project X*

"A powerful book with gripping kaleidoscopic images of war and family life, packed with painful ironies, stabbing psychological insight, metaphors that are laser-accurate, and moments of startling wisdom. In the air and on the ground, Kim Ponders delivers the fast pulse of the war experience, bringing us into that adrenaline world in which 'every moment breathed becomes an animate object, a gift.' *The Art of Uncontrolled Flight* is itself a gift, and indeed a work of art."

—Nicholas Rinaldi, author of *Between Two Rivers*

"Real romance. . . . Ponders knows of what she writes."

—*New York Post*

"Well-crafted . . . intriguing. . . . We learn here how it feels to leave the earth so drastically, and to return again with skill."

—*The Believer*

"A good weekend novel. . . . Ponders is successful in capturing the confusion and despondency her characters feel in times of war. . . . [She] knows firsthand the obstacles faced by women in the military."        —*Orlando Sentinel*

"Tense and erotic . . . urgent and morally complicated . . . this carefully crafted war story and romance marks an ambitious debut."        —*Publishers Weekly*

"Emotionally resonant. . . . Ponders is a comer. . . . This is a good read filled with the promise of even more successful sorties to come."        —*Booklist*

"Engrossing [with] gripping moments . . . shows promise."

—*Kirkus Reviews*

"Recommended. . . . A well-told story and one not often heard."        —*Library Journal*

## *About the Author*

KIM PONDERS is the author of two novels, most recently *The Last Blue Mile*. In 1989 she graduated from Syracuse University and was commissioned into the Air Force. She flew with E-3 AWACS in Saudi Arabia and Turkey during and after the Gulf War. She holds a master of science degree in international relations and a master of fine arts degree in fiction from the Warren Wilson Program for Writers. Now a speechwriter for the commander of the Air Force Reserve, she lives with her family in New Hampshire.

*The Art of Uncontrolled Flight*

# The Art of Uncontrolled Flight

A NOVEL

## Kim Ponders

HARPER PERENNIAL

NEW YORK • LONDON • TORONTO • SYDNEY

HARPER PERENNIAL

Chapter 1 first appeared as "The Art of Uncontrolled Flight," in *Chattahoochee Review*, Fall 2001. Chapter 6 first appeared as "How Bluegrass Saved My Life," in *Story Quarterly*, Spring 2003. Last seven lines from "Wings," by Susan Stewart, *Columbarium*, copyright © 2003 Susan Stewart; all rights reserved. Four lines from "The Greater Cats" reproduced with permission of Curtis Brown Group, Ltd, London, on behalf of the estate of Vita Sackville-West, © Vita Sackville-West, 1933.

A hardcover edition of this book was published in 2005 by HarperCollins Publishers.

HarperCollins books may be purchased for educational, business, or sales promotional use. For information please write: Special Markets Department, HarperCollins Publishers, 10 East 53rd Street, New York, NY 10022.

First Harper Perennial edition published 2007.

Designed by C. Linda Dingler

The Library of Congress has catalogued the hardcover edition as follows:
Ponders, Kim
    The art of uncontrolled flight : a novel / Kim Ponders.—1st ed.
      p. cm.
    ISBN 10: 0-06-078608-6
    ISBN 13: 978-0-06-078608-3
    1. Title.

  PS3616.O59A89 2005
  813'.6—dc22                            2004060729

ISBN: 978-0-06-078609-0 (pbk.)
ISBN-10: 0-06-078609-4 (pbk.)

07 08 09 10 11 ❖/RRD 10 9 8 7 6 5 4 3 2 1

*For Jacob and Seth*
*And for the memory of my mother and father,*
*whose many lives I hardly knew*

The real problem with any stall happens at the break, when the nose pitches down and the pilot's instinct is to pull back on the yoke. At low altitudes, this urge is even more extreme.

—*The Fundamentals of Flight*, "How to handle uncontrolled situations"


And if you had them forever—the forever, I mean, that is your life,
    you would still want them?
        Yes, I would want them. I would take them, so long as I could fly.

—from *WINGS*, Susan Stewart

*The Art of Uncontrolled Flight*

PART I

*Dead Reckoning*

# 1.

IN 1972, MY FATHER FLEW CARGO PLANES OUT OF Thailand as part of the operation to withdraw American troops and equipment from Vietnam. He often surprised my mother and me, returning a day or two early, and my mother would stick her sewing needle in the little battle-weary pincushion or drop the laundry basket at her feet and run to the back door as soon as she heard his boots on the stairs. Sometimes he vanished just as suddenly, leaving my mother to pick up the wrinkled laundry or finish hemming my dresses, and leaving me on the back steps with my little bag of survival gear: a compass, a chart, and a mirror. In the evenings, after the Bratsons' backyard next door had gone gray and buggy, and we could no longer see the kickball when Jeffery or Timmy sailed it over the fence, and the windows in the houses along our street grew warm with light, and the air became incensed with grilling hamburger and chicken, I sat on the back porch, watching the leaves rustling in the sudden breeze, fading contemptuously into darkness, and waited for my father to return.

We lived in the Saugausset Highlands in eastern Massachusetts—a suburb with a town common and a tiny red schoolhouse open for tours on the Fourth of July, and a cluster of colonials on narrow, frostbitten roads that led into sloping hills of two-story homes with dark paneled kitchens and big driveways for our bicycles and hockey sticks. Our own driveway was lined with mums and forsythia bushes and all sorts of lilacs that were the envy of the gardening club my mother had culled from the PTA. When my father was between rotations, she hosted dinner parties for the officers of his squadron and their wives, perhaps attempting to generate the relief and euphoria that she felt they had earned. Those evenings brought a mixture of agony and excitement, and I pulled at my mother's hips as though it might bring my father home sooner, might bring the guests and the giddiness. They never brought their children. I was allowed the run and tumble of the party, where it seemed that at the pinnacle of every chattering group, red-faced from drinking and laughing, stood my father.

"The party's an hour away," my mother said on one particular night, trying to cast me off with a glance but softening at the sight of my forehead pressed against the back screen door. "Here. Let me be." She gave me a boiled egg and some tea in her quick one-handed motion, while she seemed to do ten things with the other. She was always short with me at the crucial stages of dinner making. I assumed it was because of the timing of sauces and meats and won-tons frying on the stove. The screen door rolled off my elbow as I turned, balancing the egg and cup. She argued with herself while she cooked, as if negotiating something between the two halves of herself, the one that wanted my father home and the one that didn't. To me, it was a personal language, no more decipherable than the skitters of crickets and the Morse code of the lightning bugs. It began along with the other forest voices at about dusk, while there was still just the two of us at home. I never gave it a thought. All she ever saw from me was impatience; I saved my prettiest smiles for him.

I sat on the top step with my shoulder on the post where a hairline crack had grown every year in the three we'd lived there. It had grown faster than me, splitting the post up the middle, revealing a dark crevasse thick with spiderwebs. I peeled my egg and listened to the rising ruckus of the forest and the bugs flying in the electric lamp. As I was thinking of how the long grass near the woods must feel cool at night and be a whole different place than in the afternoons, the furious rumble of an unfamiliar engine pricked my ears, blistering the peaceful air, rolling over the stillness that had been the street. Two white eyes turned into the driveway, tight and low to the ground, with such authority that it could only be my father, home with some strange new animal of a car. Bits of eggshell scattered across my feet as I stood, only half believing the shape in the driveway that gave one final, resolute hum and went silent.

He rose from the driver's side, resting his hand where the top of the windscreen touched the open air.

I ran barefoot down the wooden steps to the cement walkway by the side of the house and leapt over a dwarf lilac onto the grass, and with two steps on the sand and pebbles of the unswept driveway, I was in his arms. He smelled of cigarettes and hard things, lifting me over his head so that he could smile up at me, the deep wrinkles set like scars around his eyes. Then I was swooping down, grounded so quickly that I felt dizzy, gripping the door of the Alfa Romeo, while my father stood, wide and magnanimous, blocking the street and the forsythia bush and everything that wasn't him, wasn't here and now and fresh.

"Take me for a ride!"

Heat rose off the hood. The car was sleek and smooth, valentine red, and the black canvas roof was tucked down behind the seats. I thought it was a gift for me. He was grinning in triumph, maneuvering my bony shoulders in the enormous girth of his hands, when his gaze lifted and his expression, without changing at all, seemed to turn cold with concern or even fear. He patted my shoulders roughly, saying, "Okay, Annie. Enough."

"Tell me," my mother said, poised in a prim, pleated skirt in the middle of the driveway, a towel twisted fiercely in her hands, "tell me the Oldsmobile broke down again and this car is a loaner."

"Hello, baby."

My mother approached with slow, dignified steps, something she'd no doubt learned as a model for Biddeford's in Austin, Texas. Her picture had appeared on the boxes of ladies' undergarments all over the South when she married the man who took her away from home forever, first to Okinawa and then to Massachusetts, where she did her best to grow sweet olive and okra (both failed) and raise a child almost entirely on her own. She had a way of gathering fury into certain points on her face. Her blossoming lips shrunk to the size of a cherry pit. Her eyes, already lined with strain, seemed to glaze over and harden like a fresco. Her forehead and cheeks were smooth and pink, never patterned with worry lines. She handled anger like she handled the garbage, with distance and composure—at least in the presence of others—and this was, I suppose, why my father sprung most of his surprises in public.

"Let me take you for a ride," he said.

She said nothing, but already the hardness was fading from her eyes and mouth. He kissed her cheek—she conceded this—and led her to the passenger door. She took her time getting situated, crossing one leg over the other and drawing her skirt over her knees. She seemed not to know what to do with her hands and finally clasped them together in her lap. My father lifted the hem of her skirt where it had fallen against the door jam. I scrambled into the space behind the seats, where there was just enough room to pull my bruised and scabby knees into the flatness of my chest and balance on the hard leather hump between my parents.

We drove along the windy roads with the trees hanging over us like arches. The wind rushed against my ears. My father drove jerkily and fast. I caught the soft, flowery scent of my mother, who was gripping the door handle for balance.

She wouldn't tell him to slow down. He drove with one hand on the stick, the other guiding the wheel in his fingers, his elbow propped on the door. His flight cap with the dip in the center stayed cocked on his head. I lifted my arm and rested it uncomfortably on the cool metal of the door, like his. I closed my eyes, felt us climbing and dipping, clipping the insides of the curves and climbing again. At the top of each little hill, I felt the momentary lightness before the car righted itself with the earth, the soft hiccup of flight.

BACK HOME, the guests were already arriving. The men, with their dark faces seeming full of gratitude for a night's diversion, stood smoking cigarettes in the driveway. The women, holding casserole dishes and plates covered with tinfoil, clustered around the blue hydrangeas in the kind of confidential chatter that always disarmed and embarrassed me. They greeted my mother warmly as she hurried by them into the house to slip on a gauzy, flowing dress the color of inchworms. The women patted and admired me. They strolled along the walkway to the back stairs, leaving a scent in their wake, complex and elusive, as though having stirred the lilacs and roses into communion. The men lingered on the back porch, my father's arm reaching around the screen door into the whiskey cabinet for glasses and a bottle.

Our kitchen became a zone of hilarious confusion, the women shouting for the whereabouts of spoons and knives, my mother shouting directions while she stood at the stove stirring hollandaise. Their jewelry clacked and rattled in percussive rhythms. They lined the hall buffet with trivets, uncovered dishes, pierced bacon-rolled scallops with toothpicks, chattered to themselves and to me, touching the top of my head and leaning down to eye level and then bouncing upright when they felt the beagle brush the backs of their legs, herself stirred from dozing on the cushions of my mother's Danish sofa.

One woman, with bright red hair and dressed in turquoise, stood a little apart from the others. She lit the candelabra on the piano and blew out the match with her pink, pursed lips. Noticing me, she leaned down and whispered, "I've heard all about you."

"Annie," my mother said, casting the two of us a glance, "there are some clothes waiting on your bed."

The woman winked at me. What had she heard? From whom?

"Annie." The look in my mother's face was stern, but she pulled me against her and kissed me on the head. "Go on, now."

I almost minded her, but the men on the porch let out a burst of laughter and their heavy shoes shuffled on the wood planks, and I slipped through the screen door into their lazy circle. They leaned on the railings and the edge of my mother's beechwood table, chasing mosquitoes with the tips of their cigarettes. My father was telling a story about two captains and a female lieutenant colonel and a phone booth. My fingertips touched the thin fabrics of their trousers, when, through the smoke and laughter, my father noticed me and said, "Annie, how'd you get out here?"

The men with their grinning, shadowy faces extended enormous hands that smelled of lemon and musk. I told them I was almost six and I was practicing to be a pilot.

"How do you practice?" one of them asked.

"I have a mirror and a compass and charts."

Sometimes in the afternoons I would lay out my instruments on the back steps, aim the center of the mirror at birds and squirrels, piercing them with a steady stream of light. The edges of the silver side were rough with old prints—mine, and maybe my father's. I spread the chart with the varying shades of brown and blue and put rocks at the four corners to keep it from curling up in the breeze, and I traced my finger along lines and numbers laid out like a code for safe passage from Saugausset to the strange, fantastic places he flew. I wanted to join with him, even in spirit, and I still believed at that point in my life, by working hard enough to crack the code of shapes and numbers in his path, that I would.

My mirror doubled as a radio. I called air traffic controllers with the kind of language my father used on the CB radio in the Delta 88. "Breaker, breaker one-nine, I'm coming in for a landing." I listened for my father, or I was my father, either way. I would come to learn that the silence from the mirror was not so different from the silence of a live frequency between transmissions, when you hope you've been heard but you're not sure, and you feel the distance between you and the rest of the world thirty thousand feet below, which is only five miles but feels like a whole continent. "That's a roger, over and out." The engines made a low, humming sound under my throat. I dialed frequencies, headings, altitudes on the compass, believing its bearings would, with time, unlock the chart's encrypted secrets, and teach me its sky language.

"Annie already knows the elements of flight." My father pulled me toward him. His breath was sharp with bourbon. "Show them, Annie, what roll is." I held my hand level with the ground and rocked it like a teetering boat.

"Pitch," he said, and I seesawed my hand. "Yaw." I spun my palm on the horizontal axis. The men clapped and cheered. On weekends, my father taught me the arc of trajectory, the role of aileron and rudder. His hands were big and calloused, and they quivered when he tried to hold them still. Trim, he explained, was a subtle application, refining the lines of the airplane's pitch. Hearing the word *trim*, I would think of the fine whiskers on the nape of his neck, the smell of Old Spice that pervaded the bathroom along with his headier smells in the morning.

"There's more," I said, but my father had risen, his great hands like a cloak on my shoulders.

"Roc, surely you're not going to teach that kid *everything* you know," one of them said, and my father laughed quietly, a complicit joke that reached me only through the tremors of his hands. "Go inside," he said, and I edged reluctantly through the small circle that had formed around us.

Dinner spooned and pitched itself onto the pearly china plates, a constant torment to the beagle who tried to snatch them from the edge of the Japanese tea table, the piano bench, the monolithic mahogany-cased stereo. My mother ate fleetingly and presided over the guests, her quick eyes alert to trouble, replacing dropped forks, freshening cocktails, complimenting the dishes brought by each of the guests. She kept the party on course, achieving the smallest of courtesies, stirring the fondue, gently retrieving a soufflé from the oven, all the time talking and laughing as though her hands were performing the most trivial of functions. It couldn't last, but she tried to prolong it until the departure of the last, late, tipsy guest, when the house suddenly rang with absent laughter, and my mother collapsed into a chair, her tumbler filled with something not water, before the arguing began.

These thoughts—these connections—did not occur to me at the time. They came later, during my own dinner parties with my husband, Dexter, an oil speculator, when we tried to mix his associates with my squadron buddies. It was the wives who did us in. The wives of the associates looked down on the wives of the flyers, and the wives of the flyers resented me for being a flyer myself and for spending so much time with their husbands. I didn't like any of them, the associates who were always pudgy and bragged about their whiskey and cast glances at my body, and their wives who laughed at everything they said, and the wives of my buddies who talked incessantly of children, and even my buddies, who acted like some decent, censored imitation of themselves until we were all turned loose on TDY—temporary duty in some distant place. But I hid my disgust in the special finger bowls I used for condiments, the cloth napkins I folded like swans.

"Relax," Dexter would say. "It's only a party."

He never understood the euphoric stakes of dinner parties, the vital illusion of satiety that comes from watching a guest consume so much of your food and wine that he can hardly stand. My mother knew. She froze ice cubes in special trays the shapes of trees and birds, small aviary collages that began to melt as soon as the whiskey was poured. Compliments from the men, when they discovered miniature arboretums in their tumblers, always pleased her. She bloomed. She presided. She could carry a conversation and keep hors d'oeuvres circulating and keep me from stealing too many furtive sips from the forgotten champagne flutes littering the tables.

"Sit by me, baby." She caught my fingers just as they were about to close upon one of the delicate stemmed glasses. But I shook loose, would not be held, and sat on the floor by my father, who could be counted on to ignore me when I slipped peeled shrimp to the dog and tasted the stirring sticks left to bleed on the napkins. The men's knees poked up from the edge of the sofa like a column of spires. I crawled under them and lay flat under the buttresses of the legs. Hidden in my private cathedral, I thought I could somehow absorb the secrets behind the stories they told and the lives they lived away from home.

One of the men gave my father a gift, wrapped in bronze-colored paper with a simple bow knotted at the center.

"What's this?" I clamored up to his knees to be part of the ceremony. He peeled back the wrapping and uncovered a picture of an F-86 (I knew it was an F-86) against a backdrop of blue sky and some land and water below. There was a shadow in the cockpit, a faint, indistinguishable glimpse of a man.

"I'll be damned," he said. It was him. I could tell by the way he admired the shot, remembering it without ever having seen it before. "I'll be damned," he said again. "That must be over Pusan. I remember, yes, it was Paul Easter took that shot one day. How did you get ahold of it?"

"Rabbit sent it," the man said. He was smiling too. He had yellow teeth and wrists that extended well beyond the cuff of his shirt. "Said it's been under his desk for three years and he's tired of kicking it."

"Rabbit," my father said, laughing. "Old Easter Rabbit. Remember that time he tried to de-ice the jet with a pickax and a broom?"

"He was a crazy son of a bitch," someone said.

*Crazy son of a bitch* was a special late-night phrase I savored rapturously.

I ran my finger across the glass to the cockpit, as though I might feel some substance behind the canopy that I could not see, but there was nothing to grab hold of, only the vague, round shape of a helmet, though I continued to press into it with my finger until my father said, "Quit, Annie," and slid me off his knee.

"We thought you'd be pleased," Zede, the redhead who'd spoken to me earlier, said. Her turquoise dress had bunched in horizontal lines at her waist as she leaned forward, grasping her knees. Zede had not arrived with a husband. She was an administrative worker in the squadron's front office, and though I would eventually know the awkwardness and suspicion that comes with being one of the few women in a flying squadron, at the time, like the other women, I resented her presence and ignored her comment.

My father ignored her too, though his face flushed, and he said, "Rabbit was a guy could stay out all night and show up in the morning with his face so gray it would make you sick just looking at him. But then he'd go out and fly the mission without so much as a tremor."

The women did what they always do when the stories begin to unfold like foreign songs from the mouths of their husbands. They sat quietly, nodding, trying to visualize the lives of their men on TDY, as though TDY were not a description but a place itself, a distinct and unfathomable place where husbands became bolder than their ordinary selves.

"What ever happened to Rabbit?" Zede asked. "Did he quit flying?" I shot her a quick look. Her calling him Rabbit seemed like a breach of etiquette, an encroachment upon the language of pilots, and it sounded rude, almost vulgar, in her voice.

"He retired," my father said. "Hey, why don't I play something? Who needs a drink?" In the general stir, as everyone reached for his glass and moved toward the piano, Zede turned to my mother and said, "So how do you like the new Alfa Romeo?"

My mother turned and looked at her with a level gaze, and smiling very slightly said, "It's a lovely car."

My father's thick fingers sank into the keys.

*He was just a lonely cowboy*
*With a heart so brave and true*
*And he learned to love a maiden*
*With eyes of heaven's blue.*

He played only the basic chords. "What do you all want to hear?" he asked, and without waiting for a reply, launched again:

*Your sweetheart waits for you, Jack*
*Your sweetheart waits for you*
*Out on a lonely prairie*
*Where skies are always blue.*

My mother turned the pages for him and begged everyone to help rescue the melody from my father's wavering voice. We sang "Juniper Jones" and "On the Brazos," then the men started into a song about a girl named Josie that was quickly silenced by the women, and I was sent to bed, where the voices came very close then drifted away, as though I were caught in a thickening bubble, and I did not wake until the arguing began.

IT BEGAN as always, in the still part of the night when even the critters and the wind had settled into sleep. It began low like the sound of clothes tumbling in the dryer and rose in sharp crests and hard syllables that exploded like crystal against a wall. There were sudden pauses—*was Annie awake?*—I forced my breath to go smooth and even. Then it rose again, building strength and pitch, until my mother unfurled her indignant wails and cries of condemnation and his voice cut through them, hard and cold as granite, and I realized, with dread, that the windows were open. I longed to get up and close them— we were better off with the sound swallowed inside our house. I pleaded with them to close themselves but did not dare to make a noise. I focused instead on silence, as though I could, being still, generate stillness.

"Annie, get up." A dream? Certainly. No. Her face looked horribly luminescent. Her hands were firm on my wrists. "Annie, get up. Get dressed."

"What's happening?" I said.

"Hurry! Get up. We're leaving."

"Where's Dad? Is the house on fire?"

"No, baby. We're going home. It's time to get up."

"Where's Dad?" I said, rising against my will. "We are home."

"Your father's not here." She hurried between my dresser and closet, grabbing handfuls of clothes. She did not turn the light on. "We're going to Texas to see your grandmother."

We crept out, furtively, like criminals. The stillness of deep night, with no sound but the click of my mother's heels hurrying like a small, frightened animal across the driveway, was awesome and terrifying. The mechanical moan of the Delta 88 seemed to object and betray us. I was too frightened to cry. We slunk down the street, though there was no one to see us but the pale tree trunks in the headlights, no one waiting to stop us, to send us home.

She still wore her party dress, a soft green flowing thing that swam in little waves at the hem. Her arms trembled through the sheer sleeves, jerking the wheel from the jouncing of potholes and the slippery inside edges of the road. The dress was tight at her throat and the rhinestone earrings dangled at her shoulders and caught the lights of passing cars. She did not look at me. Even when we crossed the bridge before the center of town and turned left and the interstate opened like a wide gray river in front of us, she gunned the engine, speeding—*speeding*—so that we left the on-ramp at seventy-five and climbing, she looked straight ahead, as though all that remained in the world lay at the end of that road.

*Eighty.*

I'd never been eighty before. The highway, rationed into lanes, ours and one on either side, seemed to fall out of existence under us, and ahead seemed to curve downward as though gravity somewhere was pulling it into the earth. I had the sense we were falling.

"Mom."

"You go to sleep," she said. "We have a long ride ahead of us."

We were alone on the road, and then in a flash we passed a Conway truck with a red cab, and then other, anonymous cars, coming upon them suddenly, like dark fish. On the side of the highway stood a bulwark of trees.

"Where are we going?"

"Home, baby," she said. "Home to your grandmamma."

Then I did start to cry, and my mother said, "Let's play a game. It's called State Lines. Pretty soon we're going to pass the state line to Connecticut, and the first one to see the sign wins a point."

I had never been to Connecticut. I kept my eyes on the signs ahead of us as they flashed out of the darkness, but they were only speed limits and littering fines.

"We're going to have to find some gas," she said.

Already we had passed several towns. It was possible to

backtrack, gas up, move on, but my mother was not about to turn around, not with her foot solid on the gas and her skin burning.

"Come on," she said, kneading the wheel. "Connecticut."

It took me a long time to understand why it was so important to get to Connecticut. After I became a pilot, I thought I had acquired the urge to fly from my father, because every time I landed in a country that he had visited, I felt I had conquered another part of him. I volunteered for any new place—Izmir, Dhahran, Rosie Roads, the Azores—and I'd be gone, gone before my husband could stop me or even ask why. I thought I was trying to catch him, but now I know, it was my mother who taught me the fine art of bolting.

"Just Connecticut," she kept saying. I kept looking for signs that would say we'd crossed the border.

We stopped twice, once in Brandon, once in Arlberry, but both times the road narrowed, dwindled into darkness. Both times we turned around in empty parking lots, retreated to the interstate. What little existed of the town was buttoned against us, barricading itself from the spectacle of my mother in her party dress and her six-year-old child.

"Please," she said. "Oh, please."

"I have to go pee."

"Just a little longer," she said in vague, encouraging tones like a dentist. "Just a little while longer."

The last place we stopped, some Esso station on the edge of a field, she said, "That's it. This is as far as we can go tonight." The air smelled of cows and mud.

"Are we in Connecticut?"

"I don't know. I don't know where we are."

She took me around the side of the gas station to squat behind a Dumpster. I peed with my back to the wall as the tips of the long grass bristled and swayed and sang in a much bolder voice than they used in the daytime.

"We can stay the night here," I said. "And get gas in the morning."

We walked back toward the car, her crisp, clicking steps and my quick, padding ones. Maybe she heard me, or maybe she wasn't listening at all. We took our places again, a sort of home from which we could think, or she could think and I could slap mosquitoes and watch how the lights of the running board turned my legs orange.

Her earrings rattled when she sunk her forehead into her fist.

"No," she said. She got out of the car and I got out too, and she said, "You stay here." She walked toward the phone booth mounted to the side of the garage. I went back to dragging the heels of my sandals against the pavement and closed my eyes, trying to remember the words to "Cowboy Jack." Night nymphs swarmed, dipping and gliding through the long grass, trying to pull me in with them. *Your sweetheart waits for you, where skies are always blue.* I fought, twisting my head to stay awake, to see him arrive in the white-eyed tiger. He would find us. We would be swept—taken—pulled back out of this land divided and pinched between roads, where towns had gathered at their corners like lint.

She came back—not exactly walking, but gliding—across the parking lot, the dress floating around her, another night nymph, caught between ground and air, phone and car, two plans launched but neither yet completed—though already my father (I realize now) would be pulling on his trousers, bidding distracted goodbyes to Zede who, sitting sprawled over her legs, begged for details of my mother's caper. We could have hidden ourselves behind the building, prolonged pursuit. It didn't have to be over, I thought. But my mother wasn't crazy enough for that. Perhaps it was enough to have made it almost to Connecticut. Perhaps she resolved next time to go farther, take a map, leave in the afternoon. Or perhaps she thought this was enough, this one run at the border, to prove she could still leave after midnight, pack a duffel, that flight was not beyond her.

I SEE HER like this now, coming forward, approaching but never arriving, a master of the hovering state. I see her framed through the slight opacity of the driver's side window. Mosquitoes skittering across my leg, willows dangling in the wind, crickets raking their legs in the grass.

It comes when my mind is as dry as the highway in Cozumel I'm walking along after hurling my wedding ring at Dexter in the parking lot of the Garden of the Reefs. The sun will surely burn my scalp to cinders, but I have left my purse in the car and have no money for a taxi, if one were even to appear on this road. Not even a mile and already the dusty residue has made my mouth sticky, and here the memory tumbles in with its fresh night air and the damp warmth of the vinyl seats and the sickness that comes when you are waiting for something and not sure what the waiting will bring.

I would have thought the night my mother and I nearly made it to Connecticut had been stitched over by the increasing number of my father's absences, mysterious calls he took with terse, one-word answers, the Easter basket given flagrantly to me by Zede that my mother kept on the dining room table but would not let me touch, and stitched over especially by my own recent marriage, falling apart in my hands like uprooted violets. After that night, Connecticut seemed like a long way off, a distinct and tangible border. I was surprised, on a trip to Texas with my father the next summer, at how easily we entered it, how there was no ceremony in crossing state lines.

Passing me in the rented red Beetle, Dexter slows, signals, pulls into the dust. He emerges from the driver's side, hands on the roof. His tanned skin shines but his shirt is not patchy with sweat like mine. My hair feels damp on my shoulders. My legs are covered in dust. At least, I think, he has seen me suffer. All suffering, I believe at this stage of my life, has a valuable point.

"Annie, will you please get in the car?"

I'm too proud and angry to speak, though I cannot explain why. We came to Cozumel to get away from the fighting, but the fighting followed us here. I never remember how it starts. All I remember, this time, is watching him flinch from the ring as if it were a weapon, and how I am both fascinated and horrified at how much I can hurt him with a diamond weighing less than a karat.

Even as I get into our rented car, I am remembering my father telling my mother in a calm voice, as he empties a canister of gas into our tank, to follow him to a station in a town thirty-five miles north. I stood and was tipsy from my battle with the field nymphs, with the soft trails of their fingers in my hair. Tears had made black patches of my mother's eyes. I felt my mother's helpless rage, watching my father feed gasoline into her tank, the gratitude she'd feel obliged to give him later, the way he'd chide her as irrational and frantic. *She's a little crazy*, people sometimes whispered in collusive tones. I knew that night she wasn't crazy. I knew she was angry and helpless.

"Get in the car, Annie," my mother said. But I was six years old and wanted to ride in the new white-eyed tiger with my father, who'd chased us down in the middle of the night and was saving us from—what? Our own foolishness?

"No," I said. "I want to ride with Dad."

"Honey," she said. "Come with me."

I climbed heavily into the car. My mother sat with her wrists hanging limp on the bottom of the wheel. My father lifted her hem from the door jam and gently closed the door. I waited until he had started the motor in the Alfa Romeo and then I jumped out of the car and ran. With one quick jerk of the door, I was sitting next to him.

"Mom said it was okay."

I knew in the general confusion, my little lie would be lost.

I was right. My mother never mentioned it. She never tried to leave again. She went back to mending my clothes and caring for me, and she died within a year from a fire started in her bedroom with a cigarette one night when my father was not at home. We moved in with Zede.

But that night she was still following us. My father kept glancing into the rearview mirror. Every now and then, his mind would wander and we'd pull away and the headlights behind us would narrow and slip into the darkness. The highway was so dark and still, it felt as though we were flying. Then he would let up on the gas and she would pull closer. I thought she would always follow us. I thought we could drive off into the night, into the darkness where everywhere was the promise of mystery, and that we could look back and she would always be there.

# 2.

ONLY IN THE FOWLER HOUSE WOULD THEY CODDLE EGGS.
"Who will coddle the egg?" Hannah yells into the den, and
Annie pictures an oval brown-shelled embryo swaddled in
tissues, clutched to a breast. Only in the Fowler house,
where the three boys—two Dartmouth grads and a pre-law
student at Suffolk (his grades didn't make the Harvard
cut)—cluster around the ottoman and arms of Annie's father's leather chair, watching the Thanksgiving game on an
old Zenith television nestled between shelves of family photos and tennis trophies. The trophies, won mostly by the
oldest son, Andrew, with a few round-robin championships
taken by Hannah and her ex-husband before the divorce,
have been jostled enough that some of the rackets have

chipped away from the hands of the smooth, gleaming bodies frozen in the moment before the forward snap of the serve. The boys' girlfriends sit on the sofa nibbling brie and olives, their glistening hair clipped in gold barrettes.

Dexter Hollis, another Dartmouth boy from Andrew's year, squats on the hearth of the woodstove eyeing the game while he flips through a picture book of the Kennedy family. Why doesn't someone answer? Surely there is an expert egg coddler in the room. Surely Hannah doesn't want Annie after shooing her out of the kitchen, waving her off with a mushroom brush, for taking up the whole sink and too carefully picking the veins from the snow peas.

Annie sits in the suede recliner between the woodstove and the mudroom, holding her wineglass—a Riedel—by the stem as the Fowlers do. She bought a wool skirt for the holiday, a coarse Scottish wrap the color of dead leaves, and it has already begun to pill. Now a run is peeking over the heel of her leather pumps. She presses her foot into the suede of the chair and nods at the girls on the sofa, a faint smile frozen to her lips. Perhaps nobody heard Hannah, or they're ignoring her. Andrew leans intently toward the television—the Patriots against Detroit. He nudges his brothers, jutting his chin and thumbing his wire-rimmed glasses up the bridge of his nose. The girls huddle together, talking collusively. Andrew's girlfriend, Alicia, sits between the other two, her hands pressed together over her skirt, a strand of pearls swaying against the thin, pastel cashmere of her sweater.

Dexter Hollis turns a page, chuckles. It seems out of the moment, but then everything does. Annie, home on a few days' leave from the Air Force Academy, can't shake the feeling that she's stepped into someone else's dream and that the dream will persist long after she's gone.

Out back, Annie's father smokes, pacing the brick patio under the trellis where the antique yellow rosebuds have snapped and withered and clutching a cornucopia of dead oak and maple leaves. They live in the eastern part of Saugausset called The Farms, on the border of the state forest, where the few remaining farms sell ice cream and riding lessons. Yesterday morning, Annie drove her father's Lincoln through the narrow, bumpy curves of the Commonway, repaved so many times that the tar laps like icing over the crab grass and wild flowers on either side, past the Holstein cows huddling over their swollen udders, through Saugausset center and into the Highlands where she used to live with her mother and father in a boxy, caramel-colored house with a finished basement. A white hatchback sat in the driveway. Her mother's shrubs had grown wild. That's all she saw before the house disappeared behind her. She drove back through the center to the Commonway, turning into the narrow back roads, cracked beyond repair and cushioned with the heavy elegance of colonials decked in dried cornstalks and pumpkins. All she had seen was a small, plain house on a shabby lawn. Wasn't that always the case with childhood, that later in life the thing itself was much smaller than memory let on?

Annie parked the Lincoln next to the old, boxy Volvo that had been passed to Hannah's youngest son, Ben. Her father had bought the Lincoln last summer from a widow in Concord. In the days before Annie left for the Air Force

Academy, she rode with him to the Saugausset Swim and Tennis Club, where he parked illegally under the pines by the gravel path to the courts until he noticed the sap spattering the ivory hood. When Annie cut the engine, it was not quite eight in the morning, but already her father was fiddling with the woodstove, grimacing as he prodded the logs with a kindling stick. He looked at her through the picture window, and his grimace deepened. She should have picked up a gallon of milk, she thought, to explain why she'd taken the car.

He'd grimaced the day before last when she'd walked into Hannah's kitchen, her A-bag slung triumphantly over her shoulder, having insisted on getting a taxi from the airport. "You're too skinny," he said, patting her jaw in a way that made her want to jerk away. "We'll have to fatten you up," Hannah said, squeezing her arm. "Do you like apple-rhubarb?"

Annie hated rhubarb, but she didn't say so. They showed her the new armchair from Cabot's. They'd gone to a hundred stores, Thomasville, Ethan Allen, finally Cabot's. He'd tried a hundred chairs. Annie tried not to think of her father systematically lowering his behind into a hundred chairs. Hannah grinned, patting the deep Aurora blue leather.

"Try it out," her father said. She sank into the lap of the chair. It was enormous. The leather felt as soft as the petals of a rose.

Then Hannah, timidly, like a teenage girl, held out her hand to show Annie the diamond, nearly two karats, brilliant cut, fastened to the band by six gold teeth. The light caught it in sparkling reds and greens, like a tiny, gleaming fish. Annie, to her own surprise and revulsion, cooed over the stone. Her father wrapped his arms around Hannah's waist and said they'd enrolled in a wine-tasting course at Harvard Extension. Annie had never known her father to drink anything but bourbon.

"HEY! I NEED an egg coddler in here!"

Past the crown molding of the doorway into the kitchen, Hannah whisks the contents of a green bowl clutched to her stomach. Her cheeks are flushed from the heat of the kitchen. Annie has never seen anyone cook so gracefully. Hannah uses strange and particular instruments when she cooks, a garlic press, a paring knife. She drinks pinot grigio with an ice cube while she cooks, though Andrew has told her the ice cube is gauche.

Annie's father grinds his cigarette into an ashtray and carries the ashtray through the french doors. When he is not looking at Hannah, his face wears the same tense, distracted look Annie has known ever since she can remember, though she can't remember much before the time her mother died, and perhaps his face was softer then. He has put on some weight since the summer. His belly sags against the girth of his trousers. He's a big man, over six feet tall. Back when he flew F-86s with the Air Force, he'd been an amateur middleweight boxer, and he still has the broad, round shoulders of a man who can duck and weave. His tennis reflexes are superb. He has large, powerful hands that leave Hannah limp when he kneads her back. Annie thinks it's this strength that attracts women like Hannah.

They think the strength goes all the way through the muscles and bone, all the way to the mind and heart.

Her father is whispering something to Hannah. Smiling, she leans toward him over the white marble counter, peeling an onion absently in her fingers, a green silk scarf falling over her shoulder. Hannah's house is the most affluent of the houses so far. There's a chandelier in the dining room and heated slate floors in the den and always in the cold months the smell of wood smoke and roasting meat in the air. Annie gets a small, silent thrill when she uses Hannah's address as her home of record. It feels indulgent, slightly dishonest.

"Annie!" He makes a clucking noise in his cheek, the way he used to call the Biddixes' horse. Her eyes float to him, but she remains frozen. "Come on, now." He jerks his head toward the counter where the egg is waiting.

"Don't bully her," Hannah says. But she doesn't protest when Annie rises, wobbling a little on the heels, trying to cover her clumsiness with a gentle smile. Sometimes when she's finally shut in the guest room, Annie feels she could extract the smile, let it hang on the crystal doorknob while her face breaths the fresh clean air of night.

WHEN ANNIE was six, her mother had dressed the Danish buffet with red velvet for the holidays. Annie remembers the ribbon candy with the delicate flavors that melted on the tongue, the canapés arranged on the Wedgwood, and her mother's elaborate earrings that dangled like a crystal waterfall in her fingers. But where was her father? She can't remember him. Even in pictures she discovered years later, after she and her father returned to the house, her mother stands in her black-and-white satin gown, one hand resting on the buffet, the fingers of her other hand treading on Annie's shoulder. She looks soberly at the camera. Annie looks away, perhaps at the beagle or at the bright bows under the tree. Surely her father took the photos, but she can't remember. He seemed always to be arriving from or departing for a mission, and the first time she remembers looking directly into his face was the night he arrived suddenly out of the darkness.

Her mother had been crying for him. She was hoarse with crying, and Annie shivered in the darkness of her room. Her mother cried often for him to come home, and when he was home, she screamed at him to leave. Annie thought it was a question of timing, that he wasn't home at the right moments, and silently begged for him to return and grant her mother a moment's peace. Sometimes Annie called for a glass of water, and her mother would arrive, patiently, trying to smooth the shaking of her voice, as if the woman wailing in the other room had been another person altogether. But this time she didn't come. There was a smell Annie had never known. She thought something awful had been left in the oven. Exasperated, confused— frightened? Was she frightened? She can't remember—she opened the bedroom door. Through a column of smoke in the hall, her mother, on her hands and knees, seemed rooted to the floor of her own room. Her red, watery eyes floated above her.

"Help me," she whispered.

Annie stumbled to the kitchen door, past the balloons

from her sixth birthday party bobbing in the smoke above the dining room table. Suddenly someone—the neighbor's daughter, Teresa—grabbed her with such force that Annie clung to her blonde hair. Teresa often sat in her boyfriend's El Camino parked in the tire tracks of the front lawn, listening to Gordon Lightfoot on the eight-track, and as Teresa carried her across the lawn, Annie thought of the songs coming from the open window, of Teresa's profile and cigarette smoke and the two feathers dangling from the rearview mirror. Her mother had warned her to stay out of the Maloneys' yard, but Annie didn't know why. She heard Teresa's boots on the cement steps and felt herself entering the forbidden house. The real fear had not occurred to her.

She spent the night on a springy bed in the corner of a room with naked walls and a velvet picture of an eagle tacked to the door. The colors of the wings and beak changed as she shifted positions, though the eyes stayed fierce and black. The door opened and her father appeared, tense and ashen-faced. She thought she had done something wrong.

She had told Teresa, hadn't she? Hadn't she mentioned her mother wavering on her knees in the bedroom?

At the funeral, her aunt and grandmother sat howling on either side of her, a distracting number of loose and crumpled tissues flowing from their two-handled purses. They smelled of gardenias, making Annie queasy. In the front row, in his Class-A blues, her father sat close to the minister and still as a stone. She thought he was gallant and strong, and she fixed her eyes on the level line of his shoulders.

Someone had given her a rose and she stood dumbly over the coffin, twirling it in her fingers.

"You were supposed to toss it," an older girl told Annie at the back of the church. Annie looked quickly back. She felt guilty holding the rose and wanted to be rid of it.

She left the rose in a doughnut shop. She had put it on the counter while she played with the apple crumble on her napkin, and a woman with cropped blonde hair and purple sunglasses came into the shop holding a lily. She handed the lily to Annie. Annie recognized her. She was the secretary of her father's squadron commander and her name was Zede.

ZEDE LIVED in an apartment with freshly painted doors and a hall that smelled of wet plaster. Annie liked to play with the brass deadbolt. She liked being buzzed in. Her mother had decorated their house with Danish furniture and art brought from their previous tour in Japan, but Zede's condo was full of strange artifacts that Annie was allowed to touch and play with: a sheepskin rug, a plastic makeup mirror with revolving lights, a wine dispenser in the shape of a heart, with a little floating tube for ice. Zede drank a kind of wine called Lancelot that came in stone carafes and tasted sweet and sparkly. Annie was allowed tiny sips.

Every morning, Annie's father drove her to school in his red Alfa Romeo and her first-grade teacher would rush to the window to watch the car (and him) depart. Annie enjoyed being singled out in this way, as if she were the reason for her father's good looks. Her father retired from the Air Force in the spring, and on summer vacation, he took her every weekday to the Merrill Lynch tower in Lowell, where he either talked to the brokers or stood in the glass-cased conference room overlooking the floor and watched the electronic ticker symbols. Usually denied lunch, Annie had nothing to do but try to make something of the bright red matrix of symbols gliding on the great banner above their heads. Her father tried to teach her to watch how the numbers went up and down by eighths. His favorites were AXP, GE, and T.

A man who had known them when her mother was alive and who had always been kind to Annie came and took her father to play tennis at his club. His name was Eddie Larkey. Her father went to the stock market in the morning, but in the afternoons, he changed his clothes and went with Eddie Larkey to play tennis. That was the new routine. A seventy-year-old retired state trooper who rode his bicycle to the club every day, his black setter-collie mix Mackey trotting beside him, Eddie had been reserving court four at two in the afternoon for so many years that all but the newest members reserved other courts and times even when his name wasn't scribbled in sharp, illegible marks across the signup sheet tacked to the equipment shed. Eddie and Annie's father rivaled for the fastest serve among the masters players, though Eddie was a good fifteen years older. Aced now and then by Annie's father, Eddie would inspect the scuff mark in the clay, rub it out with his toe, and indignantly call it wide. Everyone adored him.

Eddie taught Annie how to serve in a four-count rhythm between the toss and the snap. He let her pull his mustache. He took her to dinner at the Towne-Vue Lodge sometimes when her father had a date with Zede. She told him her mother had been alive when she ran to the door, and he had looked down through the steering wheel as if he were praying, and he had said what they always said, that it was not her fault.

THE NEXT WOMAN they lived with was named Caroline Biddix. She owned a farm in Dawson, Texas, where Annie's father had grown up, and she'd been his high-school sweetheart. She held the door open for them when they pulled into the pebble driveway under the pecan trees. Annie was eleven and Zede was long gone. The last time they'd seen her, she was screaming at them from the walkway of her pale blue apartment, where humps of mums sprung up like little turtlebacks on either side. She was telling them, or him, to get out, which Annie thought was funny, because that's what they were doing. Zede would turn back toward the door and then turn around and hurl more insults. *Selfish, self-centered son of a bitch.* It sounded like the first line of a limerick. Her father was trying to get the keys out of his pocket and get the door unlocked. By then, he was driving a powder-blue Chrysler that would talk to you when something was wrong with it. When they drove away, her father looked at her and said, "Phew," and that was the last time they ever mentioned Zede.

Caroline lived with her parents, two ancient, toothless Lithuanians, on their dying farm. She took care of them, and now she was going to take care of Annie and her father, too. She baked warm pies and made hearty meat stews. They had three chickens penned in a yard of fig trees next to the vegetable garden, and Annie chased them, trying to pin them beside the wire. The grandmother, in her hairnet and shiny hose, fussed in the garden and walked in the chicken yard plucking the pear-sized figs from the swooping branches. She steadied her thick ankles against the gopher mounds, watching Annie and mawing toothlessly at the figs.

A boy startled Annie. He stood on the bottom rung of the fence, his elbows hooked over the top. He was sucking on a blade of grass.

"How long have you been standing there?" she asked. She was breathless from the chickens.

"You don't do it right," he said. "You got to go real slow and corner them."

"You do it, then."

He shrugged and hopped off the fence, and as he was coming through the gate, Caroline came skipping out on her long, quick legs, her hair pinned in a kerchief, and kissed the boy on the head. That's how Annie met Justin, who lived with his father in his trailer every other week and was going to be her brother.

Annie's father disappeared during the day, but Annie didn't care. Caroline had a small Hammond organ in the parlor that Annie and Justin could play as loud and long as they wished. Annie helped Caroline cook and prune flowers. Caroline taught her how to pluck and quarter a chicken. Justin would bleed the birds and bring their limp bodies into the kitchen and eat pie while his mother showed Annie how to run her fingers along the downy feathers next to the skin that was still warm. It felt nothing like the cold, greasy chicken parts that came from the store. Sometimes they listened to talk shows on a radio built into the wall. The pale flowery wallpaper had been cut around it. The shows were always about Jesus.

*It's not your fault.*

Caroline had told her that also. Annie had cried dutifully, a glass of iced tea sweating on her fingers. Annie had gone to the door for help, but she had been carried away.

*Help me.* Her mother had mouthed it, Annie was sure. Teresa had grabbed her while her mother was still dying inside. What had her mother thought when Annie lingered in the doorway, then turned and ran down the hall? Annie didn't say to hang on. She didn't say she'd be back. She'd intended to come back.

Evenings at Caroline's, her father stomped heavily to the top of the lilting porch, his linen trousers damp and wrinkled. He often sent Annie the mile into town to buy groceries—ham, cigarettes, whiskey, grape soda—and because Caroline said it was safe, she was allowed to walk where she pleased. Sometimes Justin would ride her on the back of his bike, her ankles splayed out for balance, her fingers locked in the belt loops of his cutoffs. Then Caroline lit the burner and lifted the great pot full of water onto the iron stove, and Annie shucked the corn. They made stews or ham, lima beans or potatoes. Her father wrapped his arms around Caroline and sang *He was just a lonely cowboy.*

"Git!" She swatted at his hands.

He pulled the Tabasco sauce from the top of the ice box and Annie poured, standing as her mother had stood, with her hand pressed on the back of her hip. Everything else they ate could be plucked or shaken from trees, carved into slices and eaten between the thumb and the blade. As they cooked, the grandfather sat on the porch and shot at wild turkeys. Sometimes he fired into the corn, and they would find holes in the leaves, pellets burrowed into the sheaths that her father would cut out before dropping the cobs into the water. The grandmother sat on a wobbly rocker next to the grandfather, singing hymns. She lost track of things—her hairbrush, a dish, Annie's name—as though the memory of these things were too heavy to carry, but every word of "Thou Who Hath Thy Faith in the Lord" remained. Her airy voice floated through the screens, around the oak doorways, into every corner of the house, lapsing briefly with each blast of the shotgun.

After dinner, her father opened Caroline's *Collected Poems of Robert Service* to page thirty-three, dog-eared and stained with overlapping thumbprints from the sweating bourbon tumbler. They all took turns reading from "The Cremation of Sam McGee." Caroline laughed when she read it. "It's you!" she cried, falling into her father's lap. "Curse the cold through the parka's fold," he read with vigor. He said if he ever did go north again, she *could* throw him into a fire. Caroline brushed the tears from her eyes. She thought Annie's father was going to marry her.

IN BED AT NIGHT, Annie listened to all the breathing in all the parts of the house.

JUSTIN TAUGHT HER how to fish in a pond over the hill from the house. He waded waist-deep into the murky water and untangled her line. He taught her how to catch crickets and ride Calf, the chestnut Morgan. They went to the stifling four-room high school where the wooden desks smelled of paraffin and had worn in two pockets along the edge where generations of students had rested their forearms. Their teacher, Miss Maledy, spoke with a voice so soft it seemed to vanish into the walls. After school, Justin brought Annie to his bedroom in the back of his father's trailer. The fan blew shadows like frenzied moths over the veneer paneling that separated his room from his father's.

"What are we going to do when our parents get married?" Justin asked.

"Wait and see." That's what her father always said, *wait and see*. She liked waiting and seeing. It always led to nice surprises. One evening, Justin rode her home on the handlebars of his bike and watched her calves disappear in the weeds that led up to the clapboard steps, and he never saw her again.

"COSMIC," OR MAYBE, "cosmetic," one of the women on Hannah's sofa says, and the other two laugh in a delicate, trembling sort of way that Annie both despises and envies. Though her mouth waters, she turns her nose from the brie and the water crackers and glossy olives. She could gobble it up—there is enough for one decent meal—but hardly anyone has touched it. The meals here are delicious, delicate ornaments on enormous bone china plates. She fights the urge to lean grotesquely over and swipe at the cheese with the soft edge of the silver knife. No one seems to notice her restraint. Perhaps these are the kinds of manners you don't notice except in the breach. Perhaps she has passed successfully into the world of the upper middle class, where things are a little cooler than they were in her other lives, a little cleaner and more removed.

Dexter Hollis nudges Annie with the Kennedy book. *Camelot.* A Christmas present to Hannah last year from the youngest, Ben. Pictures of the Kennedy family on lawns and boats, mallets slung over their shoulders, oars in their hands—a trapped chronology of impending despair.

"Yes?"

"Check this out." He is grinning, and his voice has a fluid Southern gait not unlike Justin's.

On one page is a picture of Jack sailing away from the boathouse at Martha's Vineyard. Pictures of boatyards strike Annie as a kind of omen: people in loose cotton clothes smiling too broadly amid peeling paint and labyrinthine knots. Nobody can stay that happy for long.

The other picture, the one Dexter's tapping with his thumb, is of the young Jackie, leaning back on a swing with a pale summer dress falling over her calves, her head tilted back and smiling at the camera. She looks uncannily like Alicia, sitting on the sofa in her cashmere cardigan and black wool skirt, examining a grape she has just plucked from the cheese tray.

"Ain't it perfect?" he whispers, glancing at the girls on the sofa. They'd met briefly before the game began. She'd dismissed him as a business-hungry Dartmouth grad with some connection to the oil industry. But the observation was shrewd, something the Fowlers themselves were unlikely to grasp.

She looks at a picture above the television of the three young boys sitting on a picnic table next to a lake, Ben wearing a floppy hat and holding an oar across his shoulders, squinting and grinning into the camera. Impromptu and overexposed, it resembles the insouciant air of the Kennedys. Staring at the faces of boyish optimism and glee, she thinks, *just wait*. Nothing this good can last forever.

"Touchdown!" Andrew looks back at Dexter. "Dude, did you see that?" *Dude* sounds wrong coming from a boy who wears cashmere sweaters and gabardine slacks. He would never make it at the Academy, would never want to, and until a moment ago, Annie might have considered this her own failing.

"You guys get up and let Roc have his chair!" Hannah yells.

"No, no," he protests. "Let them be."

ANNIE'S MOTHER had brought Santa Claus to the house the year she died. Annie has a picture of herself, dressed in a pink suit with white cuffs, sitting on his lap in one of her mother's Danish chairs. Annie is looking at his face in awe. It was not her father. She suspects it was Eddie Larkey. Annie isn't sure how much of her mother she remembers and how much she gets from the pictures. She would like to ask Eddie Larkey if he dressed as Santa Claus one year, but she knows the question would make him feel sorry for her. She's supposed to have moved on by now, recognized the irrelevance of particular details.

They'd assured her, but her mother was still dying inside. Caroline had begged her father not to leave. Annie had begged him. When she went through the screen door on their last night in Dawson, he had already packed their one suitcase, a red hardback so worn it was almost pink. He glared at her, and then she knew that somehow he'd seen her with Justin. Caroline ran between them, tugging at his arm and then kissing Annie with damp cheeks. He glared at Annie, but he never said a word.

*It wasn't her fault.*

It took three days to get to Massachusetts. He drove absently, his lips sometimes forming the words in his mind, the cigarette in his fingers twitching from the maelstrom of his thoughts. Sometimes the tip of the cigarette drifted against the plush blue fabric and a burn would spread outward, like a dark stain. Annie counted the seconds before he jerked his hand up, trying to brush the ashes out of his lap and steer and get the window open at the same time. Six was the farthest she ever got.

They drove through the center of Saugausset and up the windy roads to the Highlands. Annie hadn't been in the house since the night she passed the balloons from her sixth birthday party bobbing listlessly in the smoke over the dining room table. He threw his keys on the counter, an old habit, and the noise as they slid across the gold-speckled linoleum startled them both. Most of the smoke damage had been scrubbed away from the walls, the carpet torn up, the furniture in the master bedroom removed, curtains and books and anything capable of absorbing the smell of smoke discarded, but still Annie imagined the sweet, menacing smell of burnt plaster. Her father bought a home computer, an Apple II, and set up an office on the dining room table, where the balloons had long since been removed, though she sometimes imagined the thin gray strings still knotted on the top rung of the teak chairs her mother had loved. He traded stocks over the phone until four o'clock when he poured bourbon and watched television lying on his new mattress, smoking until the freshly painted walls began to turn a yellowish gray.

Annie ruined her mother's oyster knives carving Justin's name into a corner of the back porch.

"We could have stayed," she told her father one night. "We were happy."

"I wasn't going to watch you throw your life into the dirt." That felt like a slap, but he looked at her with kindness. "You never understand the big mistakes until it's too late."

Sorting through the china that someone had wrapped in newspapers and stacked in the basement, Annie found cracked streaks of polish in the crevices of the candelabra and serving dishes where her mother had tried frantically in the last months of her life to scrub the tarnish away. A year before her death, she'd abruptly quit her afternoon naps and spent hours on the phone negotiating with contractors. She installed floor-to-ceiling mirrors in the living room and replaced the kitchen linoleum. She had the knives sharpened and polished the silver. Annie pried the chalky polish off with her thumbnail, revealing slivers of silver finish scattered like fragments of glass along the smoky surfaces.

*Help me.*

She had fled. In that way, she was no better than him.

\*        \*        \*

ANNIE REALIZES she's still holding the two halves of the eggshell, and she sets them on the floor by the woodstove. Her mother had tried to bring her father home. All she wanted was what Hannah now had.

Eddie Larkey had introduced her father to Hannah after her divorce. Annie had graduated from high school the summer her father decided to move across town. She was old enough to stay in the house alone. She was going to the Academy in July anyway, and she resolved to stay and pull out the old china and pictures her father could never bear to see. They had lived in Okinawa in the sixties, and her mother had collected tea sets and ornate dishes, strange cooking instruments, meticulous notes on gardening, and Annie wanted to explore them. But at the last moment, she changed her mind. She couldn't bear to wake up alone in the house, to find everyone gone.

Hannah took her on a tour of the great houses of Beacon Hill in Boston. It had rained, and Hannah offered to link arms with Annie under the umbrella. Annie had never imagined that such delicacy existed. She was nervous about knocking a trinket off one of the clever shelves tucked here and there. At the doorstep of each house, the tour guide would turn pertly, summoning silence, and describe what she called the house's flavor. A fine old house was just like a fine old wine, in that it had depth and distinction. By the third house, Annie grew perversely bored. She imagined her legs spread over the pile of sheets while Justin Biddix arched fiercely over her, and she wondered what the tour guide and the ladies in their rain bonnets would think of her howling, her body twisting and fighting under him.

The morning she left for the Academy, her father gave her a present, silver and turquoise earrings and a bottle of Yves Saint Laurent perfume—strange gifts, she thought, for a military cadet.

Caroline sent her care packages of cookies and socks. Three times, Annie called Justin from the pay phone in the lobby of her dormitory. He laughed with her about the tedious academics and the miles she ran in the thin Colorado air. She called her father once a week. She liked the schedule of calling him every Saturday at oh-eight-hundred hours to shrug off the petty horrors of Academy life. She told him about the tile floors they polished to a gloss with a hand rag, the beds they made so tightly that a senior cadet, during room inspections, could bounce a stack of quarters two inches off the wool blanket.

She'd gotten used to sleeping on top of her bed, fully dressed, to make the oh-five-hundred hours lineup on time. The junior cadets were hurried, harassed, and insulted at every turn. It was part of the game, Annie realized, to weed out the weak and make them resilient. Once you understood the rules, once you renounced comfort and privacy, the game was easy. It became a matter of endurance, keeping your thoughts to yourself and remaining invisible.

If Annie's sex counted against her, it was because any deviation from the norm was singled out and used for the purpose of humiliation. Annie cut her hair and ran five miles a day. She measured at twelve percent body fat, but she yearned for eight, six. Her periods vanished, which eliminated the need to hide spare Tampax in her socks. (Pocketbooks were not allowed. Pockets had to lie flat or demerits were issued.)

She marched with apparent congruity under the bold directive pronounced on the Academy wall: "Bring Me Men." She and the other dozen or so female cadets were the unrecognized exceptions to the rule. But then, she always had been, which made life at the Academy not so different from anywhere else, except that the expectations there were consistent and clear.

Her father thought she would fail. Some already had. Her roommate, a girl whose father was some FBI official, decided to leave one October morning between room inspection and breakfast. She packed and vanished without ceremony. By evening, the adjacent bed was occupied by a thin, edgy girl from Kentucky who wanted more than anything to fly C-5 transports. Annie wanted F-15s, but women were not allowed to fly fighters, and she had no particular preference among the heavy platforms. She assumed only that she would become a pilot or navigator and thought no more about the future than about the past. This was another advantage to the Academy. She became weirdly enchanted with schedules, with details, and saw how they could be used to advantage, to demonstrate competence and fill the vacancies left by an ambivalent heart.

What she missed most of all was sleep.

SHE WAS discouraged, then, to find that the chemistry of the Fowlers' den was not changed in the least by her metamorphosis, and she began to doubt that life at the Academy was in any sense real or permanent. Even Caroline, who believed in and encouraged her, was beginning to feel like an embarrassing and powerless relic. Only Justin, whose voice could stir some fresh, uncensored emotion, connected her with a resonant past. Last night, she'd called him from Hannah's formal living room, tucked in the coldest corner of the house. They didn't talk, exactly. They sat listening to the silence. She could hear him shifting, swallowing.

"Are you lying down?" she asked.

"Where are you?" he asked. She knew she couldn't make him understand.

"There's an out-of-tune piano," she said, "a basket of dried flowers in the fireplace. A porcelain leopard under the window." She could hear the television in Hannah's master bedroom. *Selfish, self-centered son of a bitch.*

"Pop shot a turkey," he said.

THERE'S A GREAT confusion before dinner, the girls running from the kitchen into the dining room with bowls of braised brussels sprouts and sweet potatoes, Annie's father carving the turkey on the butcher's block, the brothers opening bottles of wine. Even Annie has been stationed at the stove and instructed on how to stir gravy.

Andrew has brought a special treat he wouldn't reveal until now: three bottles of Gilles Perroud Beaujolais nouveau.

"May I christen your glass?" Their eyes follow the bottle as Andrew tips a smattering of wine into bowls the size of ostrich eggs. Annie finds this ritual both fascinating and a little obscene.

"Who would like a leg?" Annie's father hovers over the platter, ready to serve. On the mantle behind him is a gilded mirror and an antique clock frozen at eight twenty-four.

The wine is the color of cranberries. It tastes lovelier to her than any wine she has ever had. Much later, when she can distinguish between an Hermitage and a Châteauneuf-du-Pape, she'll recognize Beaujolais for the Thanksgiving hype that it is. But by then it will be too late. She will have lost touch with Justin and Caroline. Her father and Hannah will have moved their winter home to a gated community in Florida so that they can play on clay courts all year. Annie will think smugly of Andrew with his Beaujolais nouveau, but even he will have moved on to richer, sturdier California reds, tasting of berries and spice, that he'll call *cabs*.

"You cannot have Thanksgiving without Beaujolais," Andrew says.

"Well, I'm glad I knew that." Hannah laughs and shifts in her chair. She winks at Annie. "We've been having Thanksgiving without Beaujolais for years."

Annie's mother had polished the silver and replaced the linoleum and installed mirrors in the living room because of Zede. Her father had not been home the night of the fire because of Zede.

"Did you go to your club reunion last week?" Andrew asks.

"It's not a reunion," Hannah says. "It's just a dinner. We were supposed to go with the Sullivans, but they're not going anywhere now that Eddie's had his heart attack."

"Eddie Larkey had a heart attack?" Annie asks.

"Last Tuesday. Didn't I tell you? He's at Beth Israel."

Hannah takes a warm roll from the basket and passes it to Eric. "You ought to go down and see him, Annie. His wife is just scared to death."

"Is he okay?" Andrew asks. "He must be about eighty years old by now."

"He was playing hockey that very afternoon." Hannah pierces a cold pad of butter with the tiny two-pronged fork.

"Well, no wonder!" Andrew shoots a grin at the rest of the table.

"I guess I should have asked Colleen over for dinner," Hannah says. "But she has family."

"Is he in the ICU?" Annie asks.

Hannah nods. "There's something wrong with his lungs."

"Pneumonia?" Eric asks.

"No, some kind of fluid." Hannah waves a piece of her roll in the air. "Pulmonary something."

"Pulmonary edema," Annie says.

The table turns to Annie, an unexpected expert. She feels compelled to go on, so she adds the only detail she knows. "It happens during smoke inhalation too, but in the bronchial tubes. That's how people drown to death in fires."

It is a simple fact, but her father stares at her, pale and ashen-faced.

"My God." Andrew's face looks crumpled and horrified. She takes a sip of wine. She hadn't expected to see such emotion driven into the faces of the Fowlers.

"Poor Eddie," Ben says. "He was in such good shape."

"He's not dead," her father says. "Let's not talk about

him like he's dead."

"Nobody said he was dead," Annie says. "Haven't you been to see him?"

Her father doesn't answer. He tears a roll roughly in half and bites into it. For a moment, no one speaks and there is only the sound of his chewing.

"Well," Hannah says. "I didn't mean to sour the meal." She lifts the plate of corn and holds it out over the bowls of butternut squash and roast chestnuts. Finally, Alicia takes the plate and, with her free hand, takes the tongs and lifts an ear onto her plate.

"I love corn," she says.

Annie glances coldly at her. "Do you? Love corn, I mean."

Alicia looks at her quickly, a startled doe.

"I mean, do you really love corn? We used to grow corn." Annie is surprised to find herself talking. It had started as a joke, but the joke had not ended right. "In our yard in Dawson. Caroline's father used to shoot it with a twelve-gauge. Caroline was—"

"That's enough!" Her father is trembling with rage.

"We were happy there."

But her father is not looking at her. "Could somebody pass the wine?" he says. He inspects the words in French that he cannot read. "Andrew, what did you say was so special about it?"

"Beaujolais nouveau?" Andrew says. "It only comes out once a year."

"That's what makes it special?"

"Well, no. It isn't aged. It's bottled and shipped right

after fermentation."

"It isn't aged. That's what makes it special."

"Let me explain it to you." Andrew touches the bridge of his glasses. "There's a process called carbonic maceration. It's a fancy way of saying that one day you have a barrel of grape juice and about two weeks later you have a nice bottle of wine."

"Well, in that case," her father says, "it tastes a whole lot better than I thought it did."

The table bursts into laughter and the eating resumes. Annie wants to touch her father, but something has gone horribly wrong. He'd told her the big mistakes couldn't be seen in time. The Fowlers were nothing like the Kennedys. She'd been wrong about that, too. Nothing bad would ever happen to them.

"I brought it here for a reason," Andrew says. "We have an announcement to make."

"Oh!" Hannah says. "You don't!"

"Alicia and I are getting married."

A flurry of questions, exclamations. Annie's father is grinning, preparing to make a toast. They will marry in June, the month Annie begins survival school. The rest raise their glasses in expectation, except for Dexter, whose hand gropes absently for the glass while he stares at Annie. She has nothing to say to him, to any of them, cannot will herself to pick up her glass. Her father's toast is short and hearty. She touches the table's edge, an attempt at reconciliation that goes unnoticed. Alicia, smiling demurely, is overrun with attention. Tomorrow, Annie reassures herself, she'll be westbound for the Academy.

Ben disappears into the kitchen for another bottle.

Annie feels her fingertips on the edge of the white cloth. She thinks of Eddie lying in the dark stillness of his hospital bed. He had taught her to serve in a four-count rhythm between the toss and the snap.

"Pretend you're throwing the racket," he told her. The bristles of his mustache moved as he spoke. "Imagine you're going to hit the fence."

She had done it once, released the racket just to see how far it would fly, and she remembers that now, how she had drawn her arm back against her leg and up looping into a great wave of shoulder and elbow and wrist until the snap when she let go believing she could rattle the fence on the other side of the court, and how good the racket had felt the moment it left her hand.

# 3.

AFFAIR: A GROWN-UP WORD. FULL OF FANCY PREPARATIONS, cascading flowers, fireworks. It was a grand affair. We had an affair. They had an affair. She whispers to the mirror, parades the words, flouncing them like a boutique dress. That's really not my affair. A heady word. Too big for Annie, who still wears pink lipstick from the drugstore. Engagement and marriage had sounded equally formal, extravagant bows with disaster lurking in the laces. And now she's a veteran of all three. What's next? Divorce. The dagger word. And then back to engagement. And so we count the stages of our lives, with kids bouncing along behind us.

But affair is the chrysalis. She can already feel the transformation, the slimming. It's more real to her, more devastating, than the cancer coursing through her father's body, more consequential than the flak vest she lifts from the bedroom floor. The vest is heavy in her fingers, and she swings it around, hoists it up onto her naked shoulders. The Kevlar around the armpits is shiny and hard from wear, like a tortoise shell. In her mind, the war with Iraq has begun and she is running across some dark desert landscape, panting and desperate. The duct tape with the name SHAW A., CAPT in black letters across the chest is already beginning to peel. It's a little big. Her panties peek out of the bottom.

She turns to profile, tugs at the vest as though it were a corset. It smells of dust and antiperspirant.

"Smell that?" she declares. "Kevlar, son. I love the smell of Kevlar in the morning." Dexter, reclining on the bed, has taken notice. He sees the glow in her face, enjoys the renewed vigor with which she keeps her legs smooth, her toenails painted.

"Come here, soldier," he says.

She frowns. The show had not been meant for him. It's Jago for whom she's modeling, toward whom she's stumbling through the desert. In outward appearances, Jago is not all that different than Dexter. They both have brownish blond hair, though Jago's is cut in military style around the ears and shaved at the neck. Jago is shorter and more athletic, and he's a pilot, whereas Dexter is a geologist. Annie used to imagine Dexter on the oil rigs, the hard, grimy work he must do, but Dexter had played it down, talked more about the analysis and consulting. Jago is the aircraft commander on Annie's crew. In forty-five minutes, he will come to collect her in his red Spyder, drive her to base and pre-flight for the deployment to Saudi Arabia. It's September of 1990. The war has not yet begun, but she already sees it historically, in terms of what she has accomplished.

"Don't forget this," Dexter says. He flops onto the bed on his stomach, opens her father's old silver cigar box embossed with senior pilot's wings and lifts out her vibrator. "For peace of mind."

"Whose?"

"Mine."

She shakes her head. "We might go through customs. I'd never live it down."

"Exactly," he says. "You'd be a hero."

She laughs. "You think so? It would make a hell of a story." She takes it, a neon green scallop-shaped device he named the Grasshopper after they bought it one time in a sex shop in Dallas, and drops it into the canvas A-bag on the floor of the bedroom.

"Tampax, too," he says. "Pack plenty of Tampax to wear under your helmet."

"And condoms for storing water. But only the nonlubricated kind."

"So what was Ranger Rick doing out in the jungle with condoms, anyway?" He flops onto his stomach and shuffles the pages of her Rangers survival guide, an unorthodox collection of useful tips for the combat soldier. For three days they'd sat on the couch in sweats after Annie was put on alert, eating canned soup and pizza, watching war movies— *The Longest Day, Tora! Tora! Tora!, Apocalypse Now.* Dexter should have been offshore at one of his father's drilling rigs that week. He said it was the honeymoon they never had.

Kim Ponders

Annie laughed at that. They'd had a honeymoon, a failed, turbulent one in Cancún, where they'd both contracted diarrhea from a risky meal near Chichen Itza and Annie had panicked over second thoughts. For days, Dexter could not coax her from the shoreline, where she sat in the surf staring sulkily at the waves. Instead, he rubbed lotion on her shoulders and brought her lime-frosted glasses of rum punch.

Annie unfastens the vest, strips off her nightclothes, yesterday's bra and panties. Dexter feels the familiar urge rumbling in his boxers, but he resists it. She wouldn't take him now, squatting next to her chem gear, counting her gloves and booties, thumbing the seal on the plastic panel of the face mask.

"I should have done this before," she says.

"Relax." He sits on the bed and begins to rub the rigid muscles of her shoulders. He's a big man with strong hands, and she likes when he touches her this way, in a way that doesn't ask for anything back. "Remember to call your dad before you go."

"He's got enough to worry about," she says.

"He'd be devastated if you didn't."

Annie and Jago were flying in an exercise called Red Flag at Nellis Air Force Base, north of Las Vegas, when Iraq invaded Kuwait. They'd been there a week when there was, one early morning, an unexplained delay with the pre-mission brief. Seventy-five silhouetted, anonymous pilots and weaponeers were reclining in the darkened auditorium, legs sprawled in the walkways or over the humps of the chairs in front of them, as though their lean, tense bodies were too big for a single seat's allotted space.

"Time hack," a man's voice called in the darkness. The stage was empty, the curtain closed and illuminated by the projection lights overhead, like a theater awaiting the opening of a play.

"Who's in charge here?" called another voice, full of casual mockery. The pilots hated to be kept waiting when there was a mission to fly; they considered any delay an exasperating nuisance. Yet when the rear doors were thrown open and the room was called unexpectedly to attention, the group commander and his deputy walking briskly down the aisle, their boots illuminated in the running lights, there was an audible intake of air, a nervous focus upon the two figures cutting through the center of the audience, one dropping behind the other as they mounted the stairs to the stage.

The commander put them at ease and they folded back into their seats, sitting straighter now with their feet planted firmly in front of them. He rarely interrupted the Red Flag missions and seemed, at least to Annie, a distant, ethereal figure, the shoulders on his too-tall body slouching with years of wedging himself into an F-16 cockpit. Watching him, Annie believed that the love of flying was like any other love affair, with its raw beginning, when the feel of an airplane's controls is enough to keep a pilot awake at night, and the building into routine, when the pilot learns the airplane's strengths and weaknesses, and then later still, when he begins to love them. The commander would have watched other men—at his age, they were all men—grow older and better in their cockpits, and sometimes die in them. All of this Annie imagined. She would never have dared to approach him and ask for herself.

He told them plainly that Iraq had invaded Kuwait that morning, and that if some of them didn't understand the significance of the invasion, they soon would. Annie had never heard of Kuwait. Two slow syllables, a spondee that weighted heavily on the tongue. For a moment, she imagined it was a strange twist to the war scenario they were simulating over the Nevada desert. Its realness occurred to her gradually, with mounting significance, as the pilots and weaponeers sat stiffly digesting its suddenness. A few of them were called away immediately. They walked briskly up the ramp and disappeared into a state of being that Annie could hardly imagine. *Will we go?* she whispered to Jago, as though Jago would know the answer, as though he could grant her this one breathless wish.

The exercise continued, on a smaller if more urgent scale. Annie learned the same week, on a pay phone in the snack bar, that a malignant tumor had exposed itself in her father's right lung, metastasizing through the aorta into the dark and unpronounceable crevasses of his lymphatic system. She began to imagine identical soldiers, multiplying themselves—indeed, the estimates in the press kept growing—to overflow in the trenches lining the quiet, lung-shaped country of Kuwait.

"Why does everything have to happen at once?" she says to Dexter, turning before he can speak to pull her flight suit from the closet door.

"And what if it didn't, Annie? What if your father went into remission and Saddam marched back across the border. What would you do, then?" Dexter is working methodically at his fingernails, pushing the cuticles back with this thumb, and he does not raise his eyes to see the look of indignant contempt she will be delivering to him now.

"What does that mean—what would I do? Are you saying I'm glad my father has cancer? Do you think I like going to war?"

"It's certainly more than enough to handle, isn't it?"

"God, you're so sage, Dexter. And what would you do in my shoes?"

"Exactly what you're doing. That's the beauty of it. There's nothing else you can do." Now he does look at her. He's lying diagonally across the bed, ankles crossed, hands folded in the style of communion, like one at peace with his understanding of the world. She will remember this moment. It's one of the moments she'll call on later when she is recounting the drama of these months, the exacting penalties, the burdens and compromises of a story in which she is the uncredited hero.

"You know, you could be sympathetic with your spouse who is about to go off to war. You could be wishing me luck, cheering me on, that kind of thing."

"Oh, lord—," Dexter falls backward, laughing. "You're good, Annie. Cheer you on. I might as well wish a crocodile good luck tracking down ducks in the reeds."

Now Annie is laughing, too. "Well, that's a compliment, I guess." There's a story here, she thinks, a moral. But whose story is it, and who is listening? She gets the sense that Dexter is undermining her, and that despite it, or perhaps because of it, there's a substance growing about her persona.

Weight. She can feel it in the captain's bars on her shoulders. Glancing down sometimes, she runs her fingers over the tight blue sheen of spun silk. They seem to slope ever so slightly over the downward draft of her shoulders, as though they are too heavy to bear. She enjoys their sensation of weight and responsibility, their suggestion of wisdom.

"Captain a' captain," Jago had said to her in Vegas.

They were sitting on a bench outside the officers club at Nellis three days after the invasion was announced, watching other officers staggering out of the club, a few of them with the women who always appeared at the Nellis officers club on Fridays out of the glittery Las Vegas night. They had stopped at the bench because the night was cool and dry, and neither of them had the courage to suggest they go back to the same room.

"If this happens, it's between us, captain a' captain."

They sat watching two Navy officers chase a large prairie dog around the parking lot. One of the officers had stopped to urinate on a bush and flushed the prairie dog out of hiding. Disoriented, the creature loped in a big mound of fur across the pavement, and the two officers were leaning out of the doors of a rental car, a blue Prism, chasing it in circles.

The driver of the car had his foot outside the door. He was trying to herd the prairie dog, or kick it, or maybe scoop it up. It was weaving back and forth, and Annie feared it might veer under the tires. She considered what he meant by captain a' captain. She liked the sound of its complicity.

"My father has cancer," she told him. "He might be dying."

"Then you should go back home for a while," Jago said.

"I don't want to," she said. Some other officers, A-10 pilots, had come out of the club, and now they were hollering directions at the driver of the Prism.

"If you don't go now, you may not be able to. We're all going to be in the desert soon."

"It'll look bad if I leave now. I'll look like I'm running home." There was another fear, that if she went home she might have to stay. She might be expected to work a humanitarian assignment at a closer base. She would not be siphoned back into her father's life, not at the expense of missing a war, what might become a war.

One of the naval officers was leaning out the passenger side window, hollering, "Run, you rocky son of a bitch," to the prairie dog now making its way back into the bushy shadows at the club's edge.

"This is my home," she said. "This is my reality."

Jago said nothing. It was not his place, she supposed. She had no intention of abandoning the life she had strung together, the growing collection of TDYs and the stories she brought away from them. Nellis. Cold Lake. Rosie Roads. And now possibly Kuwait. Dexter had no idea of the life she lived out here, the narratives she pursued. She did not sleep with Jago that night, but she could see it coming, and the knowing gave her pleasure, was as delicious as the act itself.

"You know, Dex," she says, "you don't know me as well as you think you do."

"Surprise me," he says. "What don't I know."

She yearns to throw him off balance. She might tell him about the strip club, the Paradise, they went to one night in

Vegas after Killer had told a story about dropping two hundred dollars on a single dancer. He'd had to find an ATM machine. Of course they had one, he'd told the crew afterward, an ATM right next to the men's bathroom. Annie longs to tell Dexter the story, to wake in him the suspicion that there's more to her, more to her crew, than he realizes. She grins at him. The urge is intoxicating.

"What?" Dexter says. "What?"

It seems to her she has done something naughty, that she might share it with Dexter as a sort of confession, that he might be shocked at her audacity, impressed with her daring.

I'm not like other women, she wants to say. And thank God. She learned at the Academy how not to be like a woman, how not to be weak, how not to cry, how not to have PMS, or even periods, as if to be female meant to put forth a constant effusion of unpleasant secretions, as if to be a man was to withhold.

"Should I tell you?" she teases. "You promise you won't be mad?"

She had gone to the strip club more or less on a dare. Dares were, by then, routine, having been a part of everyday life at the Academy and pilot training, and were based largely on excess: exceeding a certain number of push-ups, consuming a certain number of shots. There was no fear in the dare, only in failing. Whereas in childhood games, dares always seemed to isolate—elevate—those who accepted them, in military training they had the opposite effect, tightening the fold of a community that selected its own standards. To have integrity was simply to resist swiping a classmate's clean white gloves. Real integrity, real character, was seldom tested.

So Annie had chided Killer about the ATM machine.

"Preaching from the pulpit," he mocked. They all went the following night, parked in the free lot of the Oasis across the street, and scuttled across eight lanes of traffic, arriving breathlessly in a dark hallway with neon purple running lights that reflected in the white of the manager's suit and tie. He wore a silver mermaid on his lapel and showed them around to the main room, where a girl with large, pale breasts danced to a synthetic rhythm on the peninsular stage in a circle of light. They took six swivel chairs near the front. Jago, Annie, Bear, Killer, and two young spike-haired second lieutenants from the weapons section in their first year out of the Academy who were a nuisance to Annie because they kept prodding her for reactions.

"This is a classy place," one of the lieutenants said. "Not like Butterfingers."

"They all look the same there," the other said. "Here it's like a box of Whitman's Samplers." Indeed, the girls were all different—breasty voluptuous fillies, flat-chested coeds, Asian sylphs. They all had two things in common. They were young, and they wore the same kind of necklace, tight at the neck with a thick strap of diamond-like stones lying flat along the breastbone.

"I thought it was a kind of stripper fashion," she tells Dexter, "like kimonos and geisha girls."

"And what did you think of the place?" Dexter asks.

"It was all very nonchalant. Women stripping off their clothes. All that zipping and unzipping. It was like the

Wile E. Coyote cartoon where the roadrunner and the coyote keep shedding their layers of costumes."

"So what did the boys like more, watching the girls, or watching you watch the girls?"

"That's the funny part. Everybody pretends like they're not watching anything. We're all watching each other and it's like we're standing in an elevator."

They'd barely settled in the velveteen chairs when a dark-eyed girl in a long black dress as tight as panther hide pushed herself between Killer's knees, slid out of her second skin and into her first, wearing nothing but a thong and the glimmery necklace and Killer's cool, watery gaze. He wore a blue-and-white Hawaiian shirt that made his head, even his gangly nose, look ridiculously small. Annie tried not to look priggish and flustered. She wore an expression she'd perfected at pilot training, stony observation puckered with hints of amused interest. One of the lieutenants stared openly at Killer's dancer and the other one struck a thumb at him, laughing. She'd seen plenty of kids like this who'd suffered under the severe regime of the Academy, only to go wild as weasels after graduation. The short lieutenant mocking the other one had locked himself in a tanning solarium with a girl at a house party last spring, burning his retinas nearly to blindness. He'd been grounded and had to wear eye patches for two weeks.

Annie had no such stories of her own. A male lieutenant could recover from a stupid move, but a female lieutenant would be separated and judged, her abilities questioned. Annie had kept her head down, earned her wings, and made rank quietly. But even this excursion was a risk. It would probably earn her a new call sign. Some might even start calling her a closet lesbian. The trick to being a woman in the military was to make yourself stand out, but only in a way that would leave them speechless. She'd learned this at pilot training, how to listen to the raunchy jokes and let them roll over her and then tell one that was twice as funny. As a woman pilot, you had to do everything twice as well.

"Don't let me spoil your fun," she said to Jago. He was wearing a blue polo shirt, the flaps hanging over his white shorts. She'd dressed too formally in cropped linen pants and a long silk scarf.

"Is this making you uncomfortable?"

"Are you kidding? It's like being in the locker room, except for all the men."

"You're telling me the Academy locker room looked like this?"

The girl was finished with Killer. She climbed off his lap and zipped her dress carefully over her midriff, tucking her breasts into place.

"How do they know when to stop?" Annie asked.

"When the song ends," Jago said.

"How do they know when the song ends?"

The girl flashed all of them a smile and waved and then disappeared into the dark purple light of the club.

"Any second now," Killer said, "the girls will be climbing all over Jago. It happens every time."

Annie leaned over to Jago. "Why do they all wear the same necklace?" she asked.

"You mean you don't *know*?"

Killer was right. A beautiful girl with wavy blonde hair falling nearly to her waist edged onto Jago's lap and slid her arm around his shoulders. His fingers moved gently over her leg. They might have known each other from college the way they were talking. She wore a white dress with a crocheted pattern along the breast line that reminded Annie of something Native American. His thumb beat the rhythm of the music against her thigh. Annie had watched his hands on the throttles and yoke of the E-3 and she realized she would never see them the same way again, that in the future she would glance at his hand in the process of fingering the checklist in his lap and she would remember the gentle stroking motion he was making now, just hard enough to leave a wake in the taut fabric of her dress.

"Jago here says you want to know what the necklace is for." The girl leaned over, a length of her hair falling across Annie's folded hands. She smelled intensely of vanilla.

"I didn't know it had a special purpose."

The girl smiled. She had perfect teeth. She leaned back to Jago and whispered something and Jago laughed. There was a dark-skinned girl on stage now, wearing rigid spike-healed sandals and shimmering panties. Killer and the lieutenants had split into a semicircle on the other side of the table, talking to another girl who was taking turns sitting on each of the lieutenants' laps. Bear had not said a word since they'd arrived. There was a faint flush on his cheeks, and he looked almost guiltily at Jago's girl and then at the floor when he caught Annie's gaze.

Jago and the girl evidently reached an agreement. She bent over him and shimmied out of her dress, her breasts bobbling at the tip of his nose. The girl was tanned and long-legged. Her eyes flashed and she stretched herself over him, arching and bending, running her manicured toes across his thighs. Suspending herself in the hollow above Jago's legs, she was Venus de Milo, a pearl dancing in its shell. His lips brushed the tips of her knees (though in the retelling, Annie glosses over these details, her eyes darting subversively under the sensations they elicit). Annie had never imagined Jago caught in a spell of seduction, his hands hidden in the shadow of a woman's legs, his face intent but cool, submerged briefly in the cove of her breasts, surfacing with widening eyelids, widening lips.

Was he like this at home? Annie had met Jago's wife over the summer at a squadron barbecue, a short, pretty woman with her hair pulled back, holding a toddler in one arm and a plate of miniature flag-pierced melon balls in the other. She'd set the toddler at her feet to shake Annie's hand. Annie thought jealously of her now, but then decided that Jago could not be like this in real life. Nobody could. The dancers brought it out of you.

"Now do you see how I could drop two hundred dollars?" Killer leaned toward her, grinning. She'd forgotten the others, watching Jago and the girl.

"They're not human," Annie said.

The girl was stepping back into the dress, pulling it over her body while almost imperceptibly swiping the bill from Jago's fingers. That would take finesse, Annie thought. But the girl took the twenty and pressed it back into Jago's hand and sat on his lap again.

"See!" Killer said. "See! He does this every time."

Jago said something to her and then she nodded and tucked the bill in the folds of her dress. Then she shifted her weight, smooth as a wave rolling over the sand, from Jago's lap to Annie's.

"Your friend just bought you a lap dance," she whispered.

"You're kidding," Annie said. In fact, Annie could not think of a clever way to turn the moment into her own victory. She had to either accept the lap dance or refuse it. There was no other option, no joke to make. Jago had her.

"Open your knees a little," the girl said, which made Annie go rigid. "It's okay," she whispered. "I'll take care of you."

Her skin, soaked in vanilla, felt as moist as the inside of a peach. She gently pried Annie's legs open and, to Annie's mounting alarm, ran the tender brown tips of her nipples from Annie's knees to her cheeks. Annie stayed tense, a culmination, she supposed, of years of taboo. And yet she struggled surreptitiously to touch the lengths of the girl's arms, the forbidden hips.

"You have great teeth," Annie said.

The girl touched her lips to Annie's cheek. "We have a super dental plan."

They were all, doubtless, watching this spectacle, but it was Jago she imagined. She tried to move her hands. They felt stiff and mechanical, but she managed to wrap a lock of the girl's voluminous hair in her fingers. Annie had never been cascaded in a woman's hair before, had never touched the curve of a girl's breasts. Her breath smelled like cherries. Jago was sitting so closely he could have reached over and touched them both. The girl bumped her leg, and Annie felt the hair on his calf brush against her. Then, stooping between her legs, the girl raised herself slowly, letting the stones of the necklace run like pebbles over the center of her crotch. The secret of the lap dance, Annie realized with a shock, to touch and not to touch.

The song was over. The girl gave Annie a wicked grin, and then she kissed her on the mouth, a quick kiss, but enough. Annie racked herself for a joke and came up with nothing. She didn't look at Jago.

"That was amazing," one lieutenant said.

They left soon afterward, trotting back across the highway, and Annie lifted her palms to catch the lingering smell of vanilla that hung on them thick as soup.

"You're one of us now," Killer said. She supposed she was. She did not let Jago kiss her that night. She ducked into her room and shut the door, her heart still staggering. She expected offhanded jokes the next morning, but instead, they settled into the same routine of the prebrief and mission, and nothing was said.

"That could be good or bad," she tells Dexter. "Either it was too embarrassing, and they were all talking behind my back, or it was just part of the way things are done. I guess we're not supposed to tell those kinds of stories in front of the enlisted guys."

"Decorum suddenly takes hold."

"It's like the kids pretending the parents don't have sex. In any case, I'm one of them now."

"Oh, bullshit. You're different, all right. You really think you're just another guy? Tell me something, which one of those boys wants you? Is it Jago? Or is it all of them? And don't tell me you don't know."

"It's not like that. It's not about sex. I know it sounds stupid, but you're either in or out. There's no being a woman. There's no room for that."

"You're fooling yourself, Annie, or you're fooling me. Maybe both."

Dexter is lying back with the pillows stuffed under his head, flipping his thumb on a corner of the survival guide, his hair wavy with the dampness of the shower, his face unshaven. He is, she knows, what many women call unconsciously seductive. Annie can't picture him in a strip club, his fingertips running along a stripper's seamless thigh. It seems cheap, ridiculous.

She thinks of going to the bed, touching his hair, pulling the book out of his hands. They might have one last ceremonial fling. But the thought makes her anxious. Hasn't she intentionally drawn out the exercise of packing? She could have done this yesterday. Hasn't she saved it until now to avoid a sentimental departure? Yet she wonders whether a tender farewell is taking place at Jago's house.

"And anyway, how does going to a strip club prove your worth as a pilot? Do you really think it's that daring? God, you all set the bar so low for yourselves."

"Well, let me pretend it's something. Let me pretend I'm competent, just for a little while. Jesus, I'm headed off to a war."

She might go to him, defuse the tension, but she won't. Instead, she listens to the sound of her packing, the scruffy brush of clothes landing in the canvas bag on the brown shag carpet, the drawers sliding along their runners, the empty hangers chiming *begin again begin again*. Here is something she knows: Weight and drag are negative forces. An airplane compensates with its smooth metal skin and buoyant wings. It wants to sail through the air, make itself lighter than lift. There's a simple physics here she can emulate. Reduce drag. Leave the baggage behind. Make herself a sleeker, more efficient traveler.

"You want to be a good pilot, Annie? You want to be a good officer? Forget the stunts and start making the hard choices."

"Like what?"

"Why don't you call your dad? Why don't you do it now, while you have the chance?"

She turns, examining the pockets of the room where the essential pieces of herself have been extricated. It occurs to her that her father would have seen her childhood house the same way, peripheral pieces of his own life, distinct from the vinyl toilet case and handkerchiefs packed systematically in the hanging bag, slung over his shoulder, whose plastic corners brushed the sides of the frame on his way out the back door. Of course, he wouldn't have done the packing. Her mother would have done that.

"So tell me, what else can you do with condoms?" she says. "Make an M9? Catch a camel?"

"Stop avoiding the issue."

It's the effusiveness of women that she despises, what she imagines to be effusive, and what she was told. There were damn few women in training to question that assertion, anyway, and those that were there avoided grouping, avoided the insinuations that would come with forming cliques.

"What about sand? Any uses for sand?"

"Castles," he says. "Volleyball courts. Really hard pillows. There's a section in here on how to pack. Maybe you ought to read it."

"What's that supposed to mean?"

"It means you would leave for two months with two T-shirts and twenty-five pairs of socks." He pushes off the bed and takes a brown issue shirt from her hands and begins to refold it. Straddling the A-bag, bulging beneath him like an overstuffed russet potato, he begins to scoop her clothes out and toss them on the bed. She sits, like a child, watching.

"I worry about you out in the world, Annie. You can't even pack a duffel bag." The bag deflates under him, robbed of its stuffing. She feels that packing is inconsequential, that her hands are reserved, monogamously, for the controls of an E-3. She lifts her hands, examines them, proud of them for what they know, the shapes and movements they understand.

She pulls her flight suit from the closet door and zips herself into it. Pushes her heels into the boots—scuffed beyond negligence, but it doesn't matter now—and then cinches the speed laces, wrapping them under the fold at the boot cuff. She slides the knife and the dog tags off the dresser, clips the knife to her boot cuff, drops the tags in her breast pocket. She won't wear the dog tags around her neck. Another trick she learned in UPT. They used to jingle under her bra in the hollow space between her breasts.

She'd told Dexter that story and he smiles up at her now, watching. She fidgets awkwardly to be out from under his gaze. It's a burden to be loved so much. How can he do it so openly, without fear?

"Please go call your father."

"Have you seen my water bottle?"

"Don't be so heartless," he says. But she is gone, shuffling down the hall with her flight suit, too long in the legs, dragging at her heels. She looks on top of the washer in the alcove between the hall and the kitchen, a magnet for misplaced items: old kabob spits, a roasting pan still in its original plastic, *Cooking Light* recipes clipped and forgotten, a plastic tarp used months ago to paint the kitchen lilac, a carpeted scratching post the cats rejected. Sometimes she'd like to make a forearm sweep across every surface of the house, leave the counters clean and naked, like a wing.

"You don't know my dad," she yells. "He has the constitution of a cockroach." She finds her water bottle behind the cat box, its greasy opaque plastic covered in kitty litter. She bangs it against the washer, carries it back down the hall and tucks it in the front pocket of her helmet bag. The bag is packed, the canvas squared in a taught, four-cornered rectangle. Dexter has his left sock off and his foot on the bed, fiddling with the nail clipper.

"You'd have made a great officer," she says.

"Instead, I'm just a great officer's wife. And I know your dad. Or at least I've met him, and I understand why you don't want to call. Really, I do. But I also know you'll regret it later."

Dexter rests his chin on his knee and begins to clip the edges of his toenails, pinching them into a pile at the corner of the bed. For a geologist, he's meticulous about his looks, arriving from a week in the Gulf of Mexico with the blazing, broad shoulders of a surfer and the calluses on his hands scrubbed down to the rough. She doesn't have to imagine what he'll do while she's gone. He'll be right here when she returns. Perhaps Jago is appealing for that very reason, not only because he's unavailable, but because he isn't essential.

"Do it for me," he says, "so I don't have to spend the next ten years hearing about how you never said goodbye."

"You may be right, Dex, but I'm not ready."

"You're not ready for what? Growing up? Being responsible?"

"Nope. None of those things. I've earned it."

"You don't earn negligence. It's not a reward."

"Right, it's an entitlement. That's the thing they don't teach you. You make all these sacrifices. You serve your country. You fly where they tell you to fly, and it's okay if you don't honor thy father. It's all right if you go a little crazy."

"It's all right with who?"

"With everybody. Don't you get it? It's the classic war story."

"Oh, Annie, haven't you been paying attention? In the classic war stories, the hero always loses more than he wins."

"And would you wish that on me just to prove your point?"

"It's more than you deserve." He stands now, cupping in one hand the rejected nail clippings, and pulls her to his chest. He smells warm and safe.

"What will I do without you?" She feels the emotions rising in her throat, a tight, hard nut. "I don't want it to be like this."

"Don't worry. I won't tell." Dexter kisses her forehead. She closes her eyes against him, hears the sputtering engine of Jago's Spyder pull into the driveway. "Come on, Cinderella, your motorcade is here."

He takes her hand and guides her down the hall, leaving her at the window while he returns for the bags. Jago is out of the Spyder making room behind the seats. He's shorter than Dexter and thicker in the shoulders. His jaws flex and slacken with the gum in his mouth. He looks up, his sunglasses glinting in the sun, and grins at her through the glass. She'd like to back up suddenly, go back and start the morning over and touch Dexter in a way she could remember.

He's behind her now, his hands on her shoulders. "What the hell kind of name is Jago, anyway?"

"That's his call sign. Or actually, his call sign is Jaegermeister, but everyone calls him Jago."

"Shouldn't the J be silent?" His lips are on her ear, making her squirm.

"You're dealing with the military. Listen, does the hero always have to lose more than he wins?"

He folds her inside a great bear hug, presses himself against her. "Only in the movies."

"I wish we had some time," she says.

"Just the way you like it," he says, lifting her up.

"No, no!" as he carries her over his shoulder into the recess of the living room.

Outside, Dexter squeezes her A-bag into the trunk next to Jago's. Jago swipes the sunglasses from his eyes and rounds the fender to shake his hand.

"Well, you sure look pretty," Dexter says, "but can you fight?"

Jago grins. "*Dirty Dozen*, right?"

She cannot bear to look at him. The morning has gone all wrong, and now the two men seem to be negotiating a handoff, passing her from one escort to another. She turns to Dexter, kisses him hard on the mouth and does a little backward skip toward the car, bowing awkwardly, like a puppet in a cabaret, as if to say, at last, the whole world is out of my hands.

Sings: "So long, farewell, *auf wiedersehen*, goodbye."

When the car rolls down the short driveway, it hesitates for a moment before kicking into first gear. Annie throws Dexter a secret wave, fingers stretched skyward like a child letting milkweed float in the wind. He lifts his fingers to his lips, and then they are gone.

Jago turns onto the main road. Already the wind is pulling her hair loose. There's a disquieting distance between them. He is so real, so ordinary, sitting next to her. She looks at his hands, his left on the wheel, unimpeded by a wedding ring, the other poised loosely around the gearshift. They seem to contain all his strength and potential. Touching them would be like touching the future.

She turns, the wisps of her hair whipping against her face, and yells, "Sweet farewell?"

He keeps his eyes on the road. "It was fucking hell."

She laughs, sits forward again in the rushing air. Soon they will turn northbound on the interstate with the air wrapping around the windscreen like an updraft.

# PART II

# *Decision Height*

# 4.

WE WERE INBOUND TO THE AL HUDUD CORRIDOR, THE
desert gleaming and white as a tooth, to watch for Iraqi
fighter jets while some F-16s practiced bombing runs along
the border. Christmas was four weeks away, and Jago, the
aircraft commander, sang softly on the intercom, "Men in
white dresses, and blue satin sashes. Sand storms that stay
in my nose and eyelashes."

"Oh, holy war," I sang. "The bombs are brightly falling."

Halfway out, we lost the radar and had to turn back to
the KARMA—the King Abdul Rabaal Military Arena. Killer,
the surveillance officer, had sheered seven circuit breakers
off the P57 panel with his foot while reaching under the
console for some Jolly Ranchers.

Kim Ponders

"Fucking Killer," the whole crew said.

Lieutenant Colonel Sprecht, the AWACS detachment commander, a short, nervous, balding man we called Spacely Sprocket behind his back, told us over the VHF radio to wait at the jet until he came out to inspect the damage. We all stood around in the crew compartment while Killer collected the circuit breakers and Jolly Ranchers scattered like weapon cartridges all over the blue vinyl matting. Killer wore an unauthorized go-to-war patch on his shoulder instead of the squadron eagle: a camel with a white flag in its teeth and the words FUQ IRAQ underneath. The camel dipped and bowed as he moved.

"Chimpanzees," Spacely said as he squeezed along the bulkhead, past the IFF cabinet, around the surveillance consoles where the techs were trading the corn muffins and pineapple juices from their boxed lunches. "You guys are *worse* than chimpanzees." The tabs on his flight suit were drawn snugly at the waist and wrists. His boots, despite the dust that corroded the turbines and lodged in our teeth, shined with a rich coating of Kiwi wax.

"Those things are a safety hazard," Killer said, standing up, his headset cocked behind one ear.

"Jolly Ranchers? Killer, you're a safety hazard. Take off that goddamn patch." The line of Spacely's dark hair had crept, like a retreating army, over the crown of his head, revealing a waxy orb that glistened like a dewy peach.

He began to chew his lip. "Let me ask you guys something," he said. "Do you have any idea what's going on over here? Do you have any idea what's going on *this minute*?"

Nobody answered. All twenty-one of us squeezed together over the consoles and against the curve of the port bulkhead. Jago stood next to me, twisting the cord from his headset in his fingers. He had a go-to-war patch, too, a little garden with mushrooms and the sign of marijuana and yin and yang. He wore it mainly to piss Killer off. He'd given me another patch with the word LOVE in rainbow letters, and I'd taken to wearing it on the missions instead of the one with the black-and-white radar dome and the words *I CAN SEE YOU NAKED* underneath.

Jago whispered, "Stand by for the ass-chewing."

Almost weekly, Spacely assembled all four AWACS crews, eighty mostly young men—there were only three women, a surveillance technician, a comm operator, and myself—into the trailer by the flight line that served as our ops room, in order to threaten us with Article Fifteens. Spacely was bitter at being excluded from the squadron commander's list. He had, on a check ride, allowed the copilot to pull the number three engine to idle on final approach without attempting a go-around. It was not SOP, and the wing commander, a towering man named General Giddy, sometimes hurled the brown, double-ply folders, complete with their unsigned evaluation forms, across his desk at his officers when they deviated from SOP. Spacely had been pelted with his own thick folder, redlined, and, as a final humiliation, sent to Saudi Arabia until the war began, when he would be sent back to Oklahoma into forced retirement.

"Just today," Spacely said, "this morning in fact, the UN passed Resolution 678. Anybody heard of it?"

Nobody answered. Whatever news we got came out of the *Newsweek* and *Time* magazines, weeks old, wrinkled, stained, and often ripped to pieces, that came in with the supply birds.

"That means that if the rag heads, as you like to call them, don't beat it out of Kuwait by January fifteenth—a mere twenty-eight days from now—we're all going to war."

One of the techs spit tobacco juice into a Styrofoam cup.

"Not all of us," somebody whispered.

"I've had to remind you guys that Rollerblading is not allowed at night—at any time—on the taxiway. I've counseled you about taking stray cats and other animals into your villas." Snorting arose from the surveillance section. "I've told you to stay off Perimeter Road at night, where you might be shot by the border patrol. This sounds like common sense, but not apparently to the kind of people who would hardwire a fry daddy into the galley oven. Fry daddies are, from this point forward, officially prohibited."

"Fry daddies?" I whispered to Jago. It was stifling, and my flight suit had begun to stick like cellophane to the back of my legs.

"Some idiot on crew three tried to make wings in the galley," he said. "Maintenance was mad as hell."

"Safety hazard." I nodded.

"They were just ticked that he didn't clean up the grease."

"Now," Spacely said, "there have been reports from the perimeter guards of somebody throwing rocks at the shacks. What kind of idiot would throw rocks—*at night*—at a guard holding a *loaded M16*?"

"Smarter than during the day, don't you think?" Jago whispered. His fingers were red and indented from winding through the cord of his Dave Clark headset.

Spacely swung around. His head was the color of a beefsteak tomato. "What was that, Captain Jakovitch?"

"Nothing, sir." Their eyes met, and for a moment, they looked at each other not with anger or hostility, but as though a question lingered between them, and then the question seemed to be answered, because Spacely said, "If I catch any of you out there, I'll give you an immediate Article Fifteen and send you home. Killer, if you want to make me really happy, do something like this again. Do you have anything to say?"

"It's junk food, sir. I shouldn't eat so much junk food."

"Get out," Spacely said, his lip twitching, the soft, fleshy part of his forehead pulsing. "Get off my jet. You are this close, Killer." He held up his forefinger and thumb.

On the way down the rickety wire stairs to the tarmac, Killer held up his forefinger and thumb like Spacely. "That's the size of his dick," he muttered.

"That was nice going, Killer," Jago said. "We were doing so well with Spacely and now we just might get the quarterly award for aircrew with the best attitude."

"And the best junk food," I said. As copilot, I was not expected to know much, and as a consequence, any mishap that upset the field grade staff—the higher in rank, the better—amused and delighted me. Jago, as the senior officer on the crew, had much more to lose, but that didn't occur to me at the time.

"Fuck him," Killer said. "Let's go play cards in the

hangar." He was hobbling between Jago and me trying to light a cigarette and hold his helmet bag and keep the dangling comm cord from catching fire. The cuffs of his flight suit had begun to fray and the two merit diamonds on his sleeve were gray and worn and had been sewn in lopsided, trapezoidal stitches by Killer himself when he was a young captain.

"I'm sorry about the jet, man," he said. He pinched the stub of his cigarette and dropped it in his breast pocket. The gate guard, standing in the purple shadow of his shack, waved us across the red line with the muzzle of his M16.

"I don't care, Killer," Jago said. He didn't wear any diamonds, and neither did I, but I hadn't earned five hundred hours.

"So we're going to have a holy war," Killer said.

"Do you think he was serious?" I asked. The heat burned the top of my head and singed the zippers where they rubbed against my legs. Behind us, two F-16s took off in afterburner. The noise from the engines vibrated through my ribs.

"Who knows?" Jago said. "What I want to know is, who the hell *else* is out shooting rocks at the perimeter guards."

THAT NIGHT, Jago tapped on the shutters to my room and, when I crept down the stairs into the courtyard through clusters of grass poking through cracks in the dirt, he emerged from behind a palm frond like someone out of *Casablanca*, his retractable nine-iron slung over his shoulders and a pair of night-vision goggles in his pocket.

We'd started walking out to Perimeter Road on down nights, when there was nothing to do but sit on the flat roofs drinking Dixie cups full of wine and eating Christmas cookies sent by the American schools. We made wine from yeast and sugar stolen from the chow tent, fermented in empty water bottles stolen from supply, the opening sealed with rubber gloves stolen from life support. The wine often ended up a silty, nauseating liquid the color of condensed milk. It was Jago's idea to walk out past the villas, where the Bedouins had camped before the Americans came. The villas had been built to settle the Bedouins, but they had arrived and erected their tents, sheltering their animals inside during the fierce sandstorms. On the tile floors between the electric stoves and the sinks that had never been used, you could find camel hair and smell the faint, mellow odor of dried dung.

Out past Perimeter Road, you could see nothing but the uneven land and the scattering of brush that looked, in the moonlight, like leopard spots on a velvet blue hide. Observation shacks teetered on stilts outside the rows of electrified barbed razor wire.

"You've got about seventy-five yards, Annie," Jago said. "Elbow up and look at the ball."

"I can't see a thing."

"Use these," he said, holding out the NVGs.

"I have better luck when I aim at nothing."

The rocks, good ones we'd picked up behind the East One bunker, came off the clubface with a crack. You got two points for the guard tower and one point for anything funny, like the strange, raspy grunt of a startled monitor lizard if we were lucky enough to hit one sniffing for insects along the coils of the concertina wire.

"Don't the guards ever hear us?" I asked.

"There's a thousand noises out there," Jago said. He was studying the horizon through the NVGs. Two hundred miles to the north, the Iraqi soldiers sat waiting in tanks and trenches.

"What noises?" I asked. "It's quiet as a fucking grave."

I'd forgotten a jacket, and bumps rose on my arms and legs. When the sun fell behind the horizon, the heat vanished, leaving the desert as cold and naked as a bone. I thought how the worst thing that could happen would be to crash beyond the line of sight of a radio, where the heat and the cold would pick your bones as clean and white as death.

"You're not going to believe this," Jago said.

"I can believe anything."

"Not this. You're not going to believe this." He handed over the goggles. "Over there. Ten o'clock, low."

Through NVGs, a desert is even more naked, with every shadow exposed in clear, computer-screen green and gray.

"What am I looking for?"

"Annie, are you a pilot? Look at the guard shack."

Something hovered under the shack like an eel in a sea cave. The first thing I recognized was a boot, and I followed the boot up the leg to the hip that was fleshy and bare and joined to another hip and a tangle of arms and I felt the blood leap in my chest.

"Tallyho," I said. "Two in sight."

They both had their boots on. That was the first thing you noticed. Her hair was unpinned and some of it had gotten caught in the splinters of the beam.

"The boots are what make it prime," I said.

"The boots are the best part," he said.

"Go, girl," I said. "Rock the kasbah."

"Who do you think she is?"

"I have a guess," I said. "I think it's Airman Welty from maintenance."

"I think you're right."

Jago was squinting at them through the darkness, but without the goggles all you could see was the teetering silhouette of the shack. The boards, groaning, sounded a little like a concert of monitor lizards.

"You know what I wonder?" Jago said. "I wonder who else is out here watching all this."

She used his shirt to clean herself, and then they shook the crawlers out of their pants and she clipped her hair into a bun. He put a blanket down and they crept under a part of the fence that had been cut free, and he watched as she made her way back to the road. We lay on the ground with the rocks nudging into us until she was out of sight. Then we got up and walked back to the compound without talking, except to jump and say "Sorry!" when our hands or elbows brushed together.

AFTER MORNING chow the next day, Jago, Killer, and I sat in the hangar, playing cards at a cable spool maintenance used as a table, waiting for word on the jet with the busted P57 panel. The side of the spool had dents and gouges from where maintenance had hammered and drilled through it. On the other side of the hangar sat an E-3 in chocks with electrical wires hanging out the port side and the nose cone swung down over the weather radar.

We always played with Jago's lucky pack of Russian cards he'd bought off a Greek soldier in Cyprus. Instead of suits, the cards were divided according to the units of the Soviet military, army for hearts, navy for clubs, and so forth. When you played poker, you didn't have a full house of tens and sixes. You had two T-72 tanks and three Backfire bombers. If the other guy had a straight flush, he'd lay down a whole array of surface-to-air missiles. We knew more about the Russian military from those cards than from any of the intel briefs we got in pre-mission planning.

An aluminum tile had blown loose from the roof and flapped in the hot breeze. "If we don't start this war soon," Killer said, "I'm going to have a nervous breakdown."

"Worth the delay right there," I said.

Jago squared the deck and began to deal. A couple of damp strands of hair curled over his forehead. The cards were oily. They made a smack when he slid them off the deck. Everything was slick with grime and gritty from the fine sand blowing in from the desert that ran on for a hundred miles on every side of the perimeter fence. A maintenance troop, Mo Hartley, stood on the wing of the jet in chalks, stripped down to his brown undershirt, in a nest of electrical wire.

Killer pulled a pack of gum out of his helmet bag and offered it to me. "Ladies first," he said.

"Not in this country."

"There's something so right about that," Killer said.

"Oh, that's such an old jab. You can do better, Killer."

"Cards, anyone?" Jago said. "I've got three Bears says your tanks won't make it out of Basra."

"Someone ought to make a monopoly game based on the Middle East," I said. "I'll take Kuwait City for $350 billion. You land on Kirkuk, go to prison camp."

"Come to think of it," Killer said, "you and Saudi women have a lot in common."

"How's that, Killer?" I said.

"You're both fighting the odds of a biased culture. No matter how early you get up in the morning, you're already one step behind."

"And you're fighting the last war, Killer. That's what they told us in officer training, and in pilot training, and in survival school—and yet, I'm still here."

Jago picked up the cards and started to deal again. He dealt blackjack. He had long, articulate muscles in the backs of his hands that tightened when he ran his thumb over the deck.

"And look what it costs you to be here," Killer said. "You have to fight just to stand still. Some want you to succeed. Some want you to fail. But everybody looks at you as a woman first, and that's ultimately what will keep you from being a great officer. No offense. It's got nothing to do with aptitude. The cards are stacked against you. Don't look at me like that. I didn't write the rules."

"You just follow them."

"And so do you."

Mo Hartley stood in the open doorway of the hangar, a shadow against the brightness of the ramp, shaking a cigarette from his pocket. The sun was high and it hurt to look past him at the jets. Then he stepped into the brightness and vanished in the gleaming light.

"Look," Killer said, "there are two kinds of women in the military."

"Go on, Dr. Freud."

"There's the mousy kind that follow directions well. They're competent and conservative. They make good soldiers, but not great ones. This is the kind you mainly see, women so used to adapting that they're afraid to take a stand. Then there's another kind. The kind who are out to prove themselves. They're not afraid to take a stand, and they could be great soldiers, except that they're dangerous, because they have an agenda."

"And what's their agenda?"

"To disprove misogynist bastards like me." Killer grinned, exposing a mouthful of thick, yellow teeth. "A good soldier should have only one agenda."

"To win the war."

"No. To win the engagement."

Killer rubbed the back of his neck and then felt into his pocket for his cigarettes and, remembering he was in the hangar, dropped the pack and let his hand fall on the table. "Oh, Christ, let the war start soon or I'm going to let my sores fester all over poor Annie."

"It's easy to pick on the weak," I said.

"A common war tactic."

"Except that I'm not the enemy. Unless you have an agenda."

Killer laughed. "Do you think I'm the only one who thinks like this? I'm just calling the prevailing winds. Jago will back me up."

"Oh, no, I won't."

"That's only because you've got a thing for her. Tell me how you feel about Airman Welty, Annie. Doesn't she tarnish your reputation out there fucking border guards? Isn't she setting back the reputation of your whole gender?"

"I think it eats at you, Killer, more than Annie," Jago said. "Wouldn't it be nice if you could have your pick of women and get laid every night?"

"That's easy for you to say," Killer said.

Jago kept working the cards in his hands, smoothing the edges and then snapping the corners against his thumb.

"What's that supposed to mean?" I asked.

"You know what it means."

Jago kept his eyes on the pack. "Who's in for five-card?"

"I don't know what you're talking about," I said.

"Annie, the innocent," Killer said.

"Welty's not my responsibility, any more than Jago is yours. Why are you so eager to throw stones at her and let the border guard go free?"

Killer smiled. "Ain't that how they punish adultery in this country, with stoning?"

Outside, the jets kept landing and taking off. The whine of the engine run-up made a hollow, rasping sound inside the hangar. Now, late in the day, the supply birds were starting to arrive, big lumbering C-141s and C-5s, descending into silent landings, as massive and unmanageable as clouds.

"Killer's just jealous," Jago said.

"No," I said. "Killer's right. Why don't you do me a favor and admit it." I was angry with Jago. If Killer never believes in me, I thought, I'll be a better officer, but if Jago never believes in me, I'm lost.

"Killer might be right, but that don't mean he's *right*."

"Look," I said. "Stop trying to protect me. That doesn't help." I looked at Killer. "And they don't stone women for adultery in the U.S. military, even in Saudi."

I hadn't seen Mo Hartley come back through the door and climb on the wing of the bird in chocks, and when he jumped down onto the stone floor, his boots echoed across the aluminum walls like the clap of a .38 caliber. The sound went through my heart. He brushed his hands against the side of his skinny thighs and, running his fingers through the bangs of his red hair, ducked under the leading edge of the wing. "You okay, Annie?" Jago said.

"Jesus, I'm fine," I said. "I'm perfectly fine."

Then Airman Welty walked into the hangar. She walked toward our table, and we watched her come like an apparition. The tops of her boots were creased and dusty. She walked up to us and began to tell Jago about the P57 panel. Her brown shirt was tight across her bra and her belt was cinched down over her waist. She had patches of sweat between her breasts and under her arms and she wore a Saint Christopher medallion. She had a mole on the left side of her jaw and light green eyes, and I would not have seen any of this, would not have looked twice at her, if I hadn't been privy to the previous night's exposition. Maybe she knew what we were thinking, and maybe it pleased her. Maybe it gave her a sort of power in a place where power was the main currency.

A strand of hair had stuck to her cheek and she pulled it over her ear and felt the bun at the back of her head. I didn't hear a thing she said about the panel.

"What do you want to do, sir?" she asked Jago.

"Do?"

"Do you want to come out and take a look at it or not?"

"I do. I do want to come take a look."

She looked at all of us in turn. "Well, good," she said, and then she turned and walked back out of the shadow of the hangar.

When she was past the wind strips, Jago said, "Unbelievable."

Killer was jumping up and down and panting like a dog. "Was that her? Are you sure that was her? I mean, did you *see* her?"

"Well, why don't you just go ask her," I said. "You want it both ways, Killer. You want to insult us, but you want to keep us around. It's fun to be a hypocrite." Welty disappeared in the orange sunlight. "The thing is, until you can start looking at her like any other soldier, you're no less human than us."

"Oh, human!" he cried. "Give me human!"

Outside, the heat had begun to loosen its grip. We walked out across the ramp toward the chow tent. In front of the F-16 hangar, we passed a rack of heat-seeking Aim-9s. The yellow cover had been removed from one of the missiles, and its dull black eye followed us as we passed.

"I need a shower," I said.

"Sure," Jago said. "Let's go take a shower."

"Let's all go," Killer said.

At the chow tent, we ducked under the musty flap and stood behind a bunch of British soldiers arguing about a fight—a *raugh*, they called it—one of them had started with a Saudi gate guard. The ventilation hose, duct-taped into a hole slit into the side of the tent, blew hot air and dust against our backs and onto the soldiers and airmen, officers and enlisted, who were crowded along the aluminum picnic tables with their backs and elbows rubbing against each other. We put slices of boiled ham and mustard between pieces of pita bread and took paper bowls full of cubed green Jell-O back out through the tent flap where soldiers were lining up along the boardwalk.

"It's like a regular picnic," Killer said.

Every few seconds, the tent flap opened and soldiers emerged, eating ice-cream bars and drinking bottles of Perrier. You could hear the thick clomp of their boots on the boardwalk and the flat sound when they stepped onto the street. Jago picked up a few of the stones spread outside the tent for drainage and rattled them in one hand while he held his sandwich in the other.

"What I want to know is, who is this guy in the shack and how the hell did he get her to go out there?" Killer said. "I mean, does she feel *sorry* for him?"

"It's going to torment your dreams," I said. "What was that about good soldiers having only one agenda?"

"I say live and let live," said Jago. "I'd share a foxhole with Welty any day."

"Oh, God, I'm glad I know that," I said.

"I didn't mean it that way. I was serious." He threw one of the stones at a generator draped in camouflage netting. It made a crack in the silence. Then something moved in the shadows between the generator and the net.

It was a cat. Its hind legs were lifeless and bloody. It

dragged itself from behind the generator and stopped, as if afraid to come out in the open. The skin was raw and red in patches and hung loosely over its front paws. Its fur was mealy with dirt and thistle. It had probably been hit by one of the caravan trucks that carried equipment between the ramp and the warehouses.

"Poor kitty," Killer said. The cat lay down and began to rub its cheek against the stones. Its rib cage, bare and white, jerked under its shallow breaths, but the hind legs never moved.

"We should bring it some water," I said. I looked around but all we had were the green Perrier bottles, and I thought, stupidly, that the cat wouldn't take anything with bubbles.

"What you ought to do is kill it," Killer said. "Why don't you put it out of its misery."

"Why is everything a test with you?" I said.

"It's not a test. I'm calling it like it is."

I walked over and squatted by the cat. It kept staring out past the stones and past me, as though watching death approach. Killer stood behind me.

"Help it out, Annie. A good soldier has mercy."

Jago was watching us. He was waiting to see what I would do, and I felt that either way, to kill the cat or let it live, would be a mistake, and that Killer was right to say that I would be judged first, always, as a woman, and then as a soldier.

I stood up and looked at Killer. "What do you know about mercy?"

Killer frowned at the cat. Its gray nose rested against the stones. He held his sandwich against his chest and placed the toe of his boot on the cat's skull. It made a soft, popping sound. A few tufts of the cat's hair puffed in the breeze.

"Fucking Killer," I said and walked back to where Jago was sitting. I sat, too, and picked up my sandwich.

Two tan-colored trucks passed along the road under the satellite dishes, their backs covered with canvas tarp. They were headed toward the flight line. The driver in the rear, a Pakistani with thin arms, ground the gear into place and lurched toward the one in front. Killer raised his foot to look at the bottom of his boot and then brushed it along the stones a couple of times. Jago was staring at my lap, and when I looked down, I saw the sandwich had fallen out of my hands. The stones at my feet were painted yellow with mustard.

My hands were shaking. I had never seen my hands shake before. I couldn't feel the source of the shaking, only the lightness of the fingertips against the nomex. I thought, at once, that this was a bad sign in a pilot, something Jago would remember during an inflight emergency, and I stretched my fingers out and clenched them together.

"So I guess Killer's right," I said under my breath. Jago looked at me and shook his head.

Killer took a cigarette out of his breast pocket and was trying to get his lighter started in the shelter of his hand.

"Come on," Jago said. "Let's go play Pebble Beach."

I picked up the dirty sandwich and kicked the pebbles over the smear of mustard and threw the sandwich in the trash.

"We're going?" Killer said. "We're going *now?* Hang on.

I'll be right back." He took a drag off the cigarette, dropped it on the ground, and disappeared inside the tent.

I pretended to look for monitor lizards grubbing along the fence, but I was thinking of the stillness of the cat's bones after its unceremonious death, its fur tossing fickly in the wind. Tonight something would eat it, a stray dog or magpie or lizard.

"He thinks you're tough. That's why he pushes you," Jago said. We were standing so close that I could feel the heat of his skin.

"The thing is, Jago, I know that. What I don't know is what you think."

Jago looked out past the end of the runway where two C-5s were on approach in the coral sky. "It's not that easy," he said.

Killer walked out carrying a handful of Christmas cookies. He bit into one and powdered sugar flew all over the front of his flight suit. He looked down and began to laugh.

"You coming too, Annie," he said, "or is all that beneath you?"

"I'm a pilot," I said. "Nothing's beneath me."

The light was falling. It fell very quickly at that time of year. The yellow bulbs around the hangars came on and soon the base would be recognizable only by the street lamps and the landing lights of the jets that appeared out of the darkness. We walked along the road that crossed the end of the flight line. There we would veer around the VASI lights and take the long way out to Perimeter Road to play games in the darkness, while at the edge of the base, the concertina wire rubbed in the wind like the legs of steely crickets.

# 5.

AT SOME INDISTINCT HOUR, THE DARKNESS HANGS DRAPED over the moon. The bombs fall from invisible jets. They hear them landing, the footsteps of some invading giant. Jago swings his legs off the bed, draws the curtain aside. Beyond the window, ivy scuttles the terrace. A Roman fortress sits backlit in the silent bay. The moon is burgeoning in the sky, weeping over its own creation, flooding the city and the Baghdad government buildings with light.

"Fucking McPiss," Killer whispers.

On the screen, the bombs explode from invisible planes. Pearls of fire soar, immense and intimate, over the moon-glutted streets. Babies born in Baghdad that night (and there were twenty-three) came into being under the dazzling white light streaming into the darkness, a corps of furious souls hurling themselves into the sky.

Here is the dream Killer has known, and the nightmare of not living it, of watching the new war spill into the world while he waits in a hotel room in Turkey next to a sleeping bay.

"That motherfucker," he whispers, his face submerged in the pale, flickering images of war. Bear sits at the table near the television, his lips parted, the light coming in under his teeth. Annie and Jago lean back on the headboard like an old married couple watching late-night television.

It had come unexpectedly, like a dream, and yet, like in a dream, they had known it would come. They've already forgotten how it began. The beginning has fallen back into that time before the dream began, when the war wasn't yet real, and now they are straining to see war's dark face, to grasp its ancient and horrible dimensions, not through the thing itself, but through the noisy picture on an old television screen in a Turkish hotel where, downstairs, Ukranian dancers are stripping for the clientele.

Jago stands up and looks out the window. They are weathered in at Antalya with smoke-tinged radios in the belly of their jet. They'd been directed four days earlier to make a one-day ferry flight up to Turkey to switch out a jet with their sister squadron at Incirlik Air Base. On the way back, the new communications operator, Charlie McNiff, pissed in the forward urinal, which had not been a urinal since a technical order change in 1987 had removed the basin to make room for another rack of UHF radios.

"Was he drinking?" Killer had yelled, stomping across the tarmac.

"Clearly," Jago had said.

They'd flown into Antalya through a thunderstorm with smoke and fumes in the jet, and at any other time this would have made a story. For three days, the boomers have rolled overhead, waves of cumulus fury followed by a halo of sun, and then by the cooling wind that chases the sun away and brings darkening clouds that bring the rain. They might remember this story and tell it to future friends in future bars, but now they are captives to the war, held at a distance as in a dream in which the thing you most desire is held just beyond your grasp.

"What's going to happen today?" Killer says. "Every time we take off, we get further from the fucking war."

"We'll be out by noon," Bear says.

"Maybe," Jago said. "We've got more weather coming in."

"Jesus," Killer says, "there's no justice."

*Mogadishu Somalia 01 Oct 93*

His hands have betrayed him.

He'd wanted to shake off the laziness, the whining, that was all too rampant among the people who flew big jets. After the Gulf War, he went back to Special Forces, watching the pocket wars erupting in Africa and the fringes of Europe, fault lines of the old bipolar world. Here they don't call him Killer. Here they drop him at Djibouti with enough food for three days and enough weapons to fight a small war and enough money to buy the vehicles and information they need. Their first day in Mogadishu, they take over the airfield, make a shelter out of an old hangar with a fallback position and escape route. Some of the men sleep in the Jeeps and some sleep propped against the wall. Killer drags a four-by-six wooden table away from the window because it makes him feel better to sleep off the ground.

It's nice for a while—quiet. He walks in the market without body armor, carrying only a light round. The women wear dazzling robes that look like fire next to their skin. He makes some Somali friends. They call him Ato—Slim— which is a compliment. They are very tall and their arms are as thin as the barrel on an AK-47. And black. Black as anything Killer has known. So black it's hard seeing them at night. The town is crowded and filthy, even worse than Rwanda, but the beaches are gorgeous. Some evenings, they walk there from the airfield, gather whatever wood was lying around, and make a fire. Then they lie on the pearly sand in their cutoffs and flip-flops and expensive sunglasses, watching the turquoise ocean that is so shark-infested it looks from the helicopters like salmon running to spawn. If they have beer, they drink it. Or they chew *kaat*, which makes Killer feel like he can walk anywhere without water or shoes.

Twice a week, the supply jets come in. Sometimes one of the men rides with the UN out to Beledweyne where they distribute the food. The people are calm. They gather eagerly for the bags of corn and they don't throw things.

And then the Marines come. Killer feels bad for them, coming up wet and tired on the beach in the middle of the night with the lights glaring from all those cameras. They bring reinforcements. Now you can get your hands on things like shaving cream and soap, but the Rangers are flying their Blackhawks over the UN convoys and pushing men down in the streets. Young kids who know how to fight but know nothing about how to blend in. Killer is angry because they're loud and callous and have united the whole, disparate country against them, and yet he can't see how it could have gone any other way. When the Americans start dying, he gets angry at the Somalis, too. He puts his head down and thinks about staying alive.

Nobody calls him Ato on patrol anymore. Dead men lie in the streets, their bodies splayed open like papayas. Crazy toothless women roam in the alleys. The children are slick as beans. They hurl themselves at you from rooftops and cellars and windows and cars. They come at you in dreams, from doorways you'd missed. They're young with eyes like wildebeests, or they're old and pickled with hatred, or they're so junked up on *kaat* they're ageless, immortal, and their narrowed eyes look not at you but at someplace beyond you. They want to move through you, like ghosts, and seem puzzled at the distraction of your body. They move succinctly, with fortified AK-47s, to be rid of that distraction. In dreams, his weapon is always jammed, or empty, or gone.

It bothers him that he listens to these thoughts. If he were younger he'd have dismissed them. It's bad enough that the body slows down as it gets older, but it's an even worse injustice that the mind should grow defiant, that it should begin to nag, and that the hands should listen.

The fight begins down the street between two rival clans, and Killer and the other men duck into a building to wait it out. The building is empty but there is no escape route. They wait but the shooting gets closer, and finally the other officer, a Navy SEAL, thinks they should fire just to push the fight back the other way. But then both clans start firing back, and now the seven of them are pinned in a building with grenades and GAU-4s and M9s and a Makarov that somebody'd bought in the market. Killer holds a GAU-4 with two modified drum clips of a hundred rounds each. He feels fortified. He doesn't talk when the firing starts. He wants to hear everything, and it's hard enough with all the weapons going off. The SEAL is walking from one window to the next, firing calmly, moving on. Killer, propped on his elbows, fires through a hole in the wall. He smells the carbide. He smells the sergeant next to him. He smells the trash in the alley. The men outside stand square in the street and fire back. They don't flinch at the grenades exploding behind them.

The man Killer shoots looks at the wound in his shoulder and then switches his gun to the other hand. Killer shoots him again, in the chest, and this time he falls with one arm on the gun and one arm back, wrist cocked, as though winding up for a pitch. Then Killer's gun jams, like in the dreams, and he looks down and sees that the gun hasn't jammed at all. He's out of ammunition. All he has left is a 9mm in a side holster, which he'll save in case they're forced out into the street. When he looks up, the man he shot is so close to the building that all Killer sees are his shoes. He can't get a good shot without sticking his head out of the hole, so he backs up and runs to the other side of the room leading out to the alleyway. The man lies by the side of the building with his head in the dust. Killer hates to waste a shot but he doesn't want the man to get up and come at them through a window, so he slinks out and prods the man with his GAU 4. The man has dirt in his ear, but the skin under his collar is as smooth and shiny as oil. A bloodstain has wrapped itself around his sleeve.

His hands tell him the man is dead, but he doesn't trust them. He wants to be sure. He gives the man a poke in the eye with the tip of his gun. The man absorbs the prod without protest and gives something back. Death comes up through the weapon and seizes Killer's hands, which fly up, fumbling the barrel. When the SEAL screams at him to run, he bolts. They all bolt, down the street and through the town, past the people jeering at them, clutching their empty weapons. If he had a grenade, he'd hurl it back into the street.

This is what he tells the other men at chow, and they listen, chewing.

"Wait," he starts over. "It was like this."

He wants to get it right, the mutiny of his hands, how they'd leapt back of their own. How do you discipline your own hands? How do you tell them a dead man's eye is like any other object of the inorganic world? The eye hadn't shut. That was the obscene part. It should have shut.

*Antalya Turkey 16 Jan 91*

Bear stands up and walks into the bathroom. Outside, a starless velvet blue predawn hangs over the bay, a heavy cloak so unlike the rising shade of night in Riyadh, where darkness falls away like silk. The invisible bombs are still falling, and the news anchors are starting to repeat themselves. No downed aircraft. Five Scud missile warnings, though none of them as far as Antalya.

Jago walks to the window. The thump of synthetic music drifts from the bar downstairs where the girls are busy stripping. Outside, in the bay, lies an ancient and decrepit fortress, certainly Roman, whose façade faces the hotel. To Jago, it seems like some distorted mirror on the war unfolding on the screen behind him. The war is in front of him, and behind him, but he can't see it. He can only see the burnt-out, vandalized vestiges of it echoing in the stoic face of an empty fortress.

"Stop gazing out there," Killer says. "You're driving me crazy."

He can't take his eyes from it. The windows are wide and vacant like the eyes of a jack-o'-lantern. Through them, he can see the moonlight on the sea, the same moonlight illuminating Baghdad. He thinks if he looks hard enough, he can see the war itself, taking place eight hundred miles straight south through those eyes.

Killer knows the stealth fighters are taking out all the frontline radar and communications posts, because if you can blind and mute the enemy first, he will fear what he can't see or hear, and you will rob him of his most acute sense of battle. It's the perfect war, except for one brilliant spark of blind fire, announced on TV, tentatively at first, and then with a growing sense of fresh drama, that manages to smite the belly of a stealth fighter.

"Unlucky bastard," Killer says.

Bear comes out of the bathroom. "What'd I miss?"

"Stealth went down."

This doesn't foretell the war's outcome, one downed aircraft, or ten, or a hundred, but they listen as though the bits of information relayed through the mouths of the reporters, who themselves seemed to enjoy their license to use these new words—sortie, bogie, triple A—can augur the result of a whole war.

Bear stands in front of the screen, wiping his hands on a towel.

"Get out of the way, you big moose," Killer says. Bear doesn't take his eyes off the screen, but he edges away until he is standing in the shadow of the wall, the pale light of the television flickering on his face.

*Kosovo 03 Feb 96*

Jago is flying with a NATO unit in Germany. He has a Greek copilot whose wife wraps for them perfect little triangles of baklava. There are only three Americans on his crew, the senior weapons director, himself, and a young enlisted woman, and he is the only American male. Sometimes on his way back from the head or the galley, he'll stand behind the crew seats and look at the radar screen, watching the fighters flying toward their targets. The enlisted woman is pretty, and he prefers to talk to her, but he knows he should keep his distance so there will be no confusion. Instead, he stands behind the senior director, who is tall and lanky with cropped brown hair and reminds him a little of Annie.

The real difference between Kosovo and Iraq is that here they bomb during the day. They watch a stream of fighter planes on a radar screen bomb Pristina. The weather is bad, so the bombing is taking a long time. It reminds him of watching the Turkish fighters bomb the Kurds in northern Iraq after the Gulf War in 1991. He was flying out of Turkey, then, and he would stand watching the Turkish F-4s on the radar circling around the encampments, taking their time because the Kurds had no real weapons to fight back. Then, he had watched out of curiosity as Turkey dropped its illegal weapons and returned unmolested across the American-patrolled border. Now what he feels is irritation, because as soon as the strike is finished, they can return to their base in Germany, and Jago is hungry for the dinner he hopes his wife is preparing at this moment.

The senior director is impatient, too, watching the planes and looking for a break in the clouds. She turns to Jago and says, "If this goes on much longer, I'm going to miss my son's T-ball game."

When the bombing is finished, the crew goes home. Jago's wife hasn't cooked because there is a party at their German landlord's house that night. He is tired, but he changes clothes and they go to the party, where he meets Jelena, a Serbian girl whose parents and younger brother are still living in Kosovo. He is introduced to her as an

American, and she is pleased because she speaks better English than German.

"They are bombed almost every day," she tells him. She looks sad but not desperate. They are standing in the garden behind the landlord's house. The night is warm and dry, and someone is passing around trays of ground raw pork and minced onions and shots of something that tastes like lemonade. Her family will come when there is enough money, and then her little brother will go to school again.

She is very pretty. She, too, looks a little like Annie, with her long nose and blue eyes. He would like to talk to her away from here. He'd like her to stop talking about the war.

"When will it stop?" she asks him.

"When somebody wins." He catches a glimpse of his wife talking to the landlord's daughter, who has just had a baby. His wife speaks good German, though he speaks almost none. He's curious about the life she leads, or rather, the differences in their now two distinct lives. She has stopped hinting for him to leave the service and join the airlines, and she doesn't ask him about his work anymore.

"The point is not the winning and losing," the Serbian girl says. She's leaning close to him. Jago doesn't know if it's intentional or not. "We will always fight. And pretty soon the winning won't even matter."

"The winning will always matter."

"No, you'll see. In the end, the winning is irrelevant."

*Antalya Turkey 16 Jan 91*

Dawn is emerging, like a white egg rising in oil. Who can say where dreams begin and end? Today, war is a tired horse, but at the brink of the Gulf War it was fresh and new, cleansing us of Vietnam. Jago thinks: we are living history. He is young and tantalized by glory. In twelve years, he will watch again as the fires burn in Baghdad. Marines will walk in the streets, soldiers will sit in garrison all over the Middle East like the Romans at the dark age of their empire, and still victory will duck here and there in the doorways, elusive.

He stands at the window, watching Bear and Killer make their way across the patio for breakfast. Killer chooses the table closest to the water and Bear follows, ducking his massive head under the flower pots that hang from the rafters.

Then Annie is behind him, wrapping her arms around his waist. Below them, a boy is scraping the grill, preparing it for the day, and another one is placing the fresh, white buds of flowers in teacups on the tables.

"Are we something? Or are we just part of the war?"

"What do you mean?"

"If we never went, would it be the same?"

"Would what be the same?"

"Us. Would we be the same?"

"The same as what, Annie? We're always changing. I mean, how can I answer that? How can I ever say yes?"

The fortress in the bay is as pale and gray as the sky. It's quiet now, no more ominous than the lingering sense of a nightmare. They could take the kayaks out to see it, but there's no time. In fact, there's altogether too much time, judging by the weather, but Jago prefers to keep it at a distance. He likes what it's telling him, but he doesn't quite want to be a part of it yet.

*Boston Massachusetts 12 Sept 01*

She can hear the engines of the F-15s about every 10 minutes, flying combat air patrol in pairs along a twenty-mile racetrack orbit. One will turn hot, shining its radar at the empty coastline, one will turn cold, toward the still and silent airways of the United States. On the radar of the AWACS flying somewhere (she knows) overhead, the air picture must look like what they'd imagined after a nuclear holocaust. At least they have a job to do. She envies them, up there, doing something, even if what they're doing is too late.

The Eagles are capping too low. That's the first thing you notice. They're flying low enough to be seen and heard by people in the street. Hannah looks up from the patio every time she hears one overhead. She seems to think they are different jets, all on their way somewhere.

"Where are they all going?" she asks.

"They're capping," Annie says.

"What's capping?"

"Combat Air Patrol. CAP. They should be at thirty thousand feet. They're at about ten. Do you know why?"

Annie has come to Boston on the anniversary of her father's death. She'd hoped to see the foliage and had forgotten, living now for years in southern Texas, that the foliage doesn't come until October. She and Hannah were planning a trip to her father's grave at Otis Air Force Base, but they won't be allowed in now. If her father were alive, they would talk about the operation, how all the bases would be mobilizing and the guardsmen eager to volunteer for deployment, and what route the Air Force would use to transport the Army into Afghanistan, where they would stage the operation. But as it stands, she talks of none of this, lets it jostle around in her head like a waking dream.

"Why?"

"Because they want to be seen. They're up there for us, so that we feel assured."

What Annie feels is the horror, but also (and she's ashamed of this, would deny it) the adrenaline of a war on the eve of commencement. She'd forgotten the feeling, its lightness and transience, how every moment breathed becomes an animate object, a gift. Her hands know what to do. She would like to go inside and pack her bags, fly back to the squadron and line up for mobility, but of course she won't because she doesn't belong to the squadron anymore, and anyway she is six months pregnant. The creature inside her—the terrorist, she has until now jokingly named it—kicks and sways, hiccups, sleeps with abandon.

"I hope Dexter's not worried about you," Hannah says to change the subject, or maybe to imply that Annie should go home.

"He probably is. I can't exactly fly home right now."

"Is he excited about the baby?"

"Oh, yes. He's picked out dozens of names."

"If it's a boy, you can name him after your father."

Annie looks at Hannah, though she knows Hannah is incapable of irony, of a cruelty that complex, so she lets it pass.

"Will you go to Florida this year?" she asks.

"I don't know. It's hard to think of anything right now." Hannah stands up. "I'm getting old!" she groans. She has a habit of walking stiffly, as though she's pulled muscles in both legs, though she still plays doubles tennis twice a week.

Annie sits alone on the porch where her father had spent so many hours pacing in a reverie of cigarette smoke. His spirit resounds here more than it would at any military gravesite. She'd like to talk to him about the war that will start any day, about the baby and Dexter and Jago.

*Don't make the same mistakes,* he'd say. *Don't wait until it's too late.*

*Like you did.*

*That's right.*

He was always grand on advice, fuzzy on the particulars. She thinks of the baby inside her, fears he's absorbing the words, the shock waves of a new world. How will she answer his questions when she herself is incredulous at a pair of F-15s capping at ten thousand feet in the deathly silent air over Boston? How will she explain the yellow ribbons cropping up on mailboxes and trees like the crocuses announcing spring? How the soldiers return draped in awful words like honor and sacrifice while the cameras ignore the crates that carry their bodies? And how, despite all, once you have been a soldier, it's hard to stop. A new war begins and the muscles twitch with memory. No, you say, not again, but then you are in it like an old pair of jeans, living in Qatar or Baghdad or Kandahar, and war is just another commute from home, only longer and with guns.

*Kandahar Afghanistan 06 Jul 03*

Everywhere there are guns: 9mms, M16s, the popular snub-nosed M4s with the three-round burst and compression stalk, the bad-boy fully automatic SAWs that you had to hoist over your shoulder with a thick leather strap. Bear crumbles Pop-Tarts between his lips every morning watching the Army jog around camp, singing ditties, the M16s flapping in unison over their running shorts. He was happy to see that the chaplains don't carry guns. They hold morning service in the Powerhouse. Transformers cover the roof, old wires cut and hanging from their grip. The soldiers pray with their weapons tapping against the metal chairs and afterward they drink coffee at a stand next to the old breaker closet. One morning, Bear locks weapons momentarily with a pretty Army SFC selecting a lemon cookie from the aluminum tray.

They do a little dance, disengaging their weapons. She's a small woman with round shoulders, and she carries a SAW. She smiles at him. A few cookie crumbs have lodged at the corner of her lips. Bear resists the urge to wipe them away. He says, "So do you carry the standard rounds with that or do you prefer the three-round burst?"

Later, he walks back through the compound, happy because a pretty girl has smiled at him, and he doesn't notice the argument until he's in the middle of it. Two enlisted women are yelling at each other and at one of the local interpreters standing between them.

"He touched my breast!" one of them, a buck sergeant, yells.

"You wish!" cries the other one. "You wish!"

The buck sergeant looks indignant now. The interpreter has his hands up, shaking his head. "Miss, I—"

"You saw it, Captain," she calls to Bear. "You saw him touch my breast."

Bear can't think of words for the moment. He never has the right words. It's his biggest downfall, the one for which he's most ashamed. He'd been content, and now two different women loom in front of him, breathing hard, disheveled, and an Afghan interpreter, who looks puzzled and alarmed, and they are all looking at him, as though waiting for his judgment.

"I really didn't see—"

"You saw it, sir," she cries. She's gaining confidence now. "You saw him come up and touch me. He did it on purpose."

"Please, miss," the interpreter says, clearly distraught.

Bear shakes his head, keeps walking, but the woman grabs his arm.

"Go to security with me," she says.

"Go yourself, Sergeant," he says and shakes her off. But now the interpreter has his other arm.

"They were fighting," he says, his eyes dark with fear. "I just wanted to break them up."

Bear dislikes conflict, the personal kind. A war is one thing, with guns and missiles always going off in the distance somewhere with people you never saw, but this up-close, ambiguous kind flusters him.

"Don't worry," he assures the man, and then he ducks into the communications trailer with its fresh, cool air that was always blowing on the equipment.

In the trailer, a tech sergeant Bear knows from his years in AWACS sits eating a bagel and reading *People* magazine.

"Look at this junk people read," he says, chewing. "'Jen and Ben split up.' Big deal. 'J-Lo and beau, no mo'.'"

Bear does his shift, watching the data links passing tracks to each other, listening to the requests coming over satellite radio from the air operations center in Qatar. Just before his shift ends, the captain replacing him comes in. He smells clean. He must have showered and had his clothes washed. He says, "You missed all the action. They hung some guy in the local village for touching one of our girls."

"What guy?"

"Some interpreter. They said he went after one of the Army ladies. They hung a sign under the scaffolding that said, "'Don't mess with the United States Army.'"

"But he didn't do it."

"Yeah, I know. The buck sergeant withdrew her complaint. Too late for him, though."

"What's going to happen to her?"

"I don't know." The captain shrugs. "Nothing." He sits at the table, picks up the *People* magazine. "Hey, look. Ben and Jen broke up."

Bear leaves the trailer. He examines himself, how he feels. He feels the same. This is a disappointment. He's no different than he was that morning, clacking weapons with a pretty girl in the Powerhouse. Nobody will accuse him. He is free to go to his tent, to chow, free to wander by the boneyard of scrap metal and dilapidated armory or the Blue Lagoon where they empty the latrines.

Bear has read war stories, but he always wondered what

happens to all the stories that never get told. He decides, briefly, that he will pursue this buck sergeant. He'll find her unit in the U.S. and write her commander a letter. He quickens his pace, begins to feel lighter. He'll make sure justice occurs. But how will he begin? Who will listen? Already, before he's reached the chow tent, he sees the impossibility of carrying the incident beyond this camp, beyond this very night. It can't be told. The words are there but the point is irrelevant. Instead it will live forever, a dormant war story, like a mine imbedded in his lungs, like shards of glass lodged and gleaming in his heart.

*Ramstein Germany 07 Feb 04*

"Why is it snowing in Qatar?"

"We're not in Qatar. We're in Germany."

"How long have we been in this cab?"

"About thirty minutes," Killer says. "You were dreaming." He hands the cabbie a slip of paper with the name of the restaurant. "*Donde esta?* Do you know where this bar is?"

The streets are dark, but they look familiar. Jago recognizes the church and the Italian place run by the Greek family and the ice-cream stand whose Rolladens are shut for the night. He thinks he is still dreaming, and then he realizes he used to live in this village.

"I got divorced right around here."

"I'm sorry, man."

"It's okay. The thing is, sometimes I forget."

Killer opens the window a crack. "Smoke?" he asks. "*Fume?*"

"Why do you keep speaking Spanish?"

Killer taps the cigarette against his temple to get the cab driver's attention. "*Ja?*" The cabbie nods.

"They speak Italian in Somalia. They speak Russian in Tajikistan. They speak German in Vincenza. Why wouldn't they speak Spanish here?"

Jago got divorced two wars ago. It was an amicable divorce, and he sees his kids, Chris and Todd, now eight and five, on a flexible basis. He remembers their birthdays by which war he was fighting that year.

"There's some kind of *gasthaus*," Killer says.

"No kidding."

"I don't have the address. Name. *Nombre. Die Schion.*"

"*Ich weisse das nicht.* I don't know it," the cabbie says.

"Did you hear about Annie?" Jago asks, suddenly.

"Annie Shaw?"

"Remember Thumper? He ran into her, I forget where, San Antonio, I think. He was in Qatar."

"Annie?"

"No, Thumper. She's having a baby."

"Thumper?"

"No, Annie. Thumper was the engineer on our AWACS crew, don't you remember?"

"Sure. He played the banjo."

"No, that was Bear. That was the navigator."

Killer and Jago had hooked up in Qatar. Jago was on his way back from Liberia. He was tired and weak and surprised that nobody was talking about the war there. Killer had run some air raids over Kirkuk from a computer in the air operations center in Qatar, following directions he received in a chat room by a source he knew only as "National."

That was in Jago's dream. They were both standing in the air operations center watching the infrared picture off the AC-130 Spectre gunship's combat camera piped over satellite onto a plasma screen. Killer was passing intelligence from National up to the Spectre. On the screen you could see three white bodies huddling over the hood of a pickup truck. You could hear what they were saying, and they were speaking English, so Jago knew it was a dream.

One said, "Let's go into the trees." There were trees here, in the Iraqi desert of Jago's dream.

Another said, "I know where there's a forest. It's in a secret place."

Jago was the only one who could hear their voices, and he tried to relay what they were saying to Killer, but Killer was busy talking to the Spectre pilot on the radio. He wanted to tell them not to shoot because it might be important to know where the forest was, and anyway he was curious about where they could hide a forest in the desert. In the dream, he is leaning toward Killer, has his hand on his shoulder, when the firing starts, the rapid bursts of a Howitzer. Then the bodies were lying flat on the ground, and just like in real life, the bodies stayed light for a while, and then they went out, like candles.

"Here it is," Killer says. "I remember this place."

"What are their names?" Jago asks.

"One is Sanya. I don't know the other one."

Jago is embarrassed about his fingernails. The nerves in his fingertips are so shot he can barely tie his boots anymore. The dirt has been wedged under the nails for six months. It won't come out. He tried a wire brush once, which felt like the tingling of a hairbrush, and drew blood from his fingers, but the dirt wouldn't go away.

Killer pays the cab driver and they go into the restaurant, and there are two girls sitting at a thick, wooden table waiting for them. One of the girls is Jelena. Her hair is shorter but Jago knows her immediately.

"Where is your family?" he asks.

"My parents are here," she says. He doesn't ask about her brother. Instead, he puts his arm around her shoulders. He feels very tender, like he should protect her, and also like he's known her for years, and that he's been planning this reunion all along.

"Are you all right?" she asks.

He feels shaky and weak, and he is wary of his emotions in this state. He's thinking of how things go around in circles. If he had not fought the war in Kosovo, he would not have met this girl at the party, nor would he have been divorced. The war brought both. They were both inevitable. But it was more than that. The war in Kosovo had brought the girl here, to him, just as the war in Liberia had brought him to her. He had worried for a time that Annie was the one, that he had lost his opportunity, but Annie was pregnant now and somewhere in the United States living the kind of life he vaguely remembers, the ways one remembers primary school.

"I'm tired," he says.

"We're between wars right now," Killer is telling Sanya.

"Where will you go next?" Sanya asks.

"Back to Iraq. Maybe Iran. North Africa. China. Outer space."

"I'm sick, actually," Jago says.

"Someday we'll fight wars from space," Killer says. "No people, except for the enemy. Just lasers and beams of things. And the Army. You always need the Army, someone to do the inhabiting. Smoke?"

"You were right," Jago says to Jelena. "About the winning. After a while, it doesn't matter."

*Antalya Turkey 16 Jan 91*

They walk through the dining room where the waiters are lining the buds of little white and yellow flowers in teacups on the tables. Bear is eating a boiled egg wrapped in slices of meat and cheese, and Killer has pushed his plate away and is smoking and watching the fortress in the bay. Local men are already on the patio sipping *Efes* and playing backgammon. The backs of their hands are dirty, and they wear trousers with thick collared shirts buttoned against the dampness. They all stop what they are doing to look at Annie as she passes.

"*El Capitan*," one of them says, smiling with gaps between his teeth.

"*Nescafe*," Jago calls to the waiter and makes a circling motion with his finger. The beach is empty, the sand moist from the rain.

"We're out at noon," Jago says.

"There is a god," Killer says.

Jago turns his face to the sky. Annie watches him: he does this on the ramp, too, before the preflight. He figures the direction of the lowest wind and stands with his back to it, and he finds the highest clouds and judges how they're moving across the three-nine line of his shoulders. Then he says there's weather coming, or this is all going to clear by tomorrow, and almost always he's right. He does the same now except that the wind is coming right to left over the bay, and he judges the cirrus to be the highest clouds, with fallstreaks beginning to trail out to the east.

"We'll get some clear before the rest moves in," he says. Annie can't see it, hasn't yet learned to read the weather by sight, but the moment she hears him, she imagines the gray beginning to burn off, the blueness take over the bay, though none of this has happened yet.

"It's like the night before Christmas," Annie says. Jago looks away. Killer taps his cigarette on the railing.

"We should go out now," Killer says, "just to be set with everything."

Jago nods. "Go check out."

"Why are you in such a hurry?" Bear asks.

"Because I'm tired of looking at your sloppy face."

In the bay, the fortress hovers mutely over the dark water. Jago wants to pull one of the kayaks off the railing and paddle out to it, and he can't figure out why the urge is so strong, what it could tell him up close that it can't reveal at a distance. And then he realizes, he wants to stand on top of the ruins, he wants to walk through the archway, to stroll the ramparts, to play the part of a claiming hero, the most recent victor. He doesn't want to understand it. He just wants to own it.

"Let's go, man," Killer says. "Stop daydreaming."

There's a general rustling at the table. Sitting is no longer bearable. Annie can sense a shift in the urgency. They stride across the patio and she no longer sees the civilians playing backgammon, even as they look up with their dirty, cracked fingers on the wooden pieces, to watch the American officers on their way to win the war.

# 6.

BEAR HAD A FIVE-STRING BANJO WITH A REINFORCED NECK.
Sometimes I held it and plucked at the strings, and it made
a twangy, unhappy sound, but he could make it sing. His
whole face listened as he played and his wet, pink lips
moved silently over the words. On night sorties over the Al
Jarha corridor, he would fold up his maps, and in the thirty
minutes between checkpoints, he would slide his banjo out
from under his console and twist around so that the neck
would sometimes poke Thumper, the engineer, in the side.
He played left-handed. Jago and Thumper and I would listen and sip coffee, watching the fires in Kuwait burning like
the eyes of a hundred animals in the dark.

Sometimes on the outbound, the comm operator would

tune up the BBC International on the high-frequency radio, and news of the war would come to us as we were flying in it, as though we were already a part of history. With its static and whirls, the radio sounded like a 1950s sci-fi show. The war did not feel like a part of us. On the ground, I felt naked and slow, but in the air, I felt secret and anonymous, buttoned inside our metal skin.

Bear carried his banjo everywhere. He kept a snapshot of his pedigree Saint Bernard, Jo Dick, on his console during missions. Bear and Jo Dick had the same round, hungry eyes. Bear's girlfriend, Candy, had her arms around Jo Dick in the picture that was taken outside Bear's duplex in front of the wheel from his king-cab. Candy also had a soft, round face with wet lips and freckles that matched the auburn fur on Jo Dick's ears, but Bear always made it clear that the picture was of Jo Dick and not of the girl.

"See," he would say. "Here's my pup."

And whatever crew dog he was talking to would always say, "Which one?"

Bear was a Congregationalist Baptist, and on Sunday mornings, if there wasn't a mission, he would attend the "meetings," as we had to call them, in the big sand-colored tent in the middle of the compound. This gave Jago and me an hour and a half alone in their room. We would lie in bed, my unpinned hair stretching in tendrils across Jago's stomach, the sheets blown half across the floor like a parachute, and watch the light come through the shutters and form slats on the opposite wall. The shutters were always closed, so even when the sun was high and full, the room was dark and cool as dusk.

"Let's get married," I would say.

"If we do it in Saudi, does that mean I'll own you?"

We were already married to people back home, but we didn't talk about them or the letters they wrote us or the photographs we kept hidden in the back of our aircrew aids. His wife's name was Pam, and Jago had introduced her at a Fourth of July squadron picnic. We tried to shake hands, but she was balancing, on one arm, a tray of melon balls pierced with miniature American flags and, on the other, a little boy dressed in orange swim trunks. I could remember little about her except her short, practical hair and stocky legs (she had been a competition water skier), and that we looked nothing alike.

Bear tried to stay out as long as he could. He went to his meeting, where from under the canvas flaps you could hear someone banging away at a piano, and then he went to chow and then to check the mail, but I was always still there when Bear came noisily into the villa. He would sit around in the living room picking at his banjo while I collected my clothes and crept out. An hour or so later, I'd arrive again, knocking on the door. Bear would have picked up my mail for me. Jago would have showered, and I would smell the dampness and want to rush up to him and put my hands on his wet hair and fresh clothes, but instead we would all sit around on the floor of the common room, feeling awkward and embarrassed.

One night, we were playing Pigs on the floor of their villa with a British Jaguar pilot and a Turkish NATO intelligence officer. The Brit's name was Heppotok. He was half Greek. He wore an olive green canvas jacket as old as World

War II that hung halfway down his thighs. His hair was thick and black and his eyes were as dark as obsidian, and he tried to wrap me in his gaze as though it was a rich mink blanket. He'd traded his stash of tempazepam for some distilled Kentucky bourbon that arrived in kingdom through the wheel wells of a KC-135, and he kept splashing mouthfuls of it into our waxy paper cups.

The Turk, whose name was Sedami, was overweight and smelled awful, but he was kind, and he kept offering us the dates he'd brought to eat with the bourbon.

"The convoy looked like a snake," the Brit said. "A big-bellied anaconda with scales made of lights, winding out of Kuwait, its body stalled and trying to push the head faster."

"Where were you guys heading out of?" Bear asked.

"Where were we heading *out of?*" the Brit asked. He was grinning and drunk. Bear was waiting for him to answer. He didn't seem to understand what the Brit had found amusing. "We were heading *out of* Dhahran. Straight off, you saw the head advancing toward Basra."

Jago spit some tangerine seeds into an empty Skoal can. Bear went back to absently plucking his banjo, the arm of it resting on his shoulder like a cello.

"The only question," the Brit said, "was where to drop the first round."

"That's a beautiful story," Jago said, and I laughed so hard that I had to look away.

Jago, lying back on his elbow, swallowed the whiskey in his cup and then reached forward and brushed his thumb lightly over my toes. Everyone noticed this but the Brit, who kept describing the run over the Basra highway and swaying forward, trying to capture me in his deep luminous eyes. He was very drunk.

"Beautiful." The Brit wagged his head. "More like fantastic."

"Sedami was there," Jago said. "Was it fantastic, Sedami?"

Sedami raised his eyes. He'd been studying the two small plastic pigs in his hands that a marine had given him in Jubail after he'd surveyed the damage from the Basra highway bombing. Sedami had ordered one of the corporals to go around and shut off the music still playing in some of the Jeeps that had been blown off the road. The corporal had climbed out of the charred and mangled openings in the Jeeps where the doors had been, holding his cap over his eyes and retching. The Marine had dropped the pigs in Sedami's hand after hearing the story about the Basra highway because the Marine had had nothing else on him to give.

"Please," Sedami said. "It's not important."

The Brit weaved, eying him hotly. "What's not important, chap?"

Sedami grinned and shook his head. He was doing mandatory service in Brussels when the war started, and now he only wanted to finish his tour and go home to his fiancée, a civil engineer from Ankara.

Bear said, "I wouldn't think pigs were the right kind of thing to give a Muslim."

Sedami laughed. "He didn't mean it that way."

"It was perfect idiocy," the Brit said. "The Basra highway lit up like a festival. The first time we hit them, they all wisely shut their lights off. But they turned them on again, fanning out from the middle, like they were all connected by a power grid. I can't for my life understand why."

Jago rolled onto his back and began to gargle his whiskey. His fingers, holding a date, circled in the air over his mouth.

"Anyway," Sedami said. "I am Zoroastrian. Not that he would have known."

Jago swallowed his whiskey. "I didn't know there were any of those left."

"You all think it was a slaughter," the Brit shouted. "It *was* a slaughter. But they were *armed*, don't you understand? They were shooting at us, and then they turned their lights back on. Why in God's name did they turn their fucking lights back on?"

Jago dropped the date into his mouth and waggled it between his teeth.

"You have no idea," the Brit said. "You AWACS guys, *eyes of the sky*, lumbering around in the Hindenburg two hundred miles from the nearest missile. You think you can shake your head at the fighter pilots who do the nasty work. No offense."

"We all do the nasty work," Jago said.

We were supposed to be celebrating. The end of the war was near and we were all going to be going home. But it didn't feel like we were going home. It didn't feel like we were moving at all.

"How about you guys kiss and make up?" I asked. With that, the Brit began to leer and sway in my direction again. "You're a small guy," I said. "That's why you get drunk so easily."

"Small hands, warm heart."

I think he said "heart," but I'll never know, because as he spoke, the room shook as though he had spit thunder out of his mouth. The floor trembled as if a clapper had struck the body of a tower bell housed in the walls. The sirens began to howl. A blast shot through my eardrums and nerves. We became a frantic flock of hips and elbows, sifting and sorting the chem gear in our trembling fingers.

"What's here?" Sedami yelled.

The blast itself answered, a second one, again like the clapping of a great bell surrounding us, piercing at first and then succumbing to a deadening hum. I tripped over a sleeve. The Brit yelled. I saw his lips move. I saw the sound leave his mouth. It seemed to shimmer and dissipate in the air. I was still falling backward into Jago, bent at the hips. He had lifted his elbow to steady me. The air was thick and gray, and I seemed to be diving through it, and then my shoulder hit the ground. Something snapped. I thought it was the banjo. I pulled a nylon bag out of the way, and then I saw that it was not the banjo I'd broken, but my own gas mask. The canister felt loose, like a broken bone, under the hood.

Sitting on my shins, I lifted the straps off the face plate and unfolded the hood, and the canister fell out in my hand. It had fractured in a clean line. I kept trying to fit the canister against the air nozzle, and it kept falling out in my hand.

"Is there any duct tape?"

The hum of a struck bell still filled the room. Sedami slid his canvas belt off and they tried to strap the canister on by wrapping the buckle around my neck.

"Take mine," Jago said, ripping his mask off. His face was flushed and the imprint of the rubber had begun to form along his jaw.

"Don't be stupid," I said.

The Brit was fumbling with his booties. He had put his rubber gloves on and the fingertips kept getting caught in the laces.

"I'm ordering you to take it."

"You're *ordering* me?" He was trying to push the mask into my hands. Bear was grunting and waving his hands at us, his oversuit bunched like fishing gaiters at the waist. I tried not to think of the pictures they had showed us of blackened and bubbling skin. I hoped death would come quickly, without too much thrashing.

"You're not brave," Jago yelled. His face was purple. "You're stupid."

"I'm not the one holding a perfectly good mask in my hands."

I wanted to take the mask more than anything, but I would not. If I took the mask, Jago would sit and think about Pam and the little boy with the orange swim trunks.

"Don't make me do this," he said.

I turned from him and began to put on the oversuit and the booties and the cotton and rubber gloves. I didn't look at him again until I was sure the mask was over his face. He was breathing hard. I could see the sweat glistening in the corners of his eyes.

Sedami had put some M8 tape on the wall to sense nerve or blister agents, but no one looked at it. He made a motion that I should put my mask on anyway. I shook my head. The mask was no good without the canister, though I understood it would make them feel better to see me wearing it.

My eyes stung. I sniffed for the smell of almonds and fresh-cut grass. They were all trying not to stare at me, and I pretended to be alone in the room, looking at anything except their faces, pale as prairie dogs in the shadows of the masks. I shut my eyes. It occurred to me that I didn't really know any of them. It would be horrible to die in front of these huffing strangers. It would be humiliating.

I saw that Jago would go on living, go back to Pam and the little boy, and then I saw that he would do this regardless of whether I lived, and it made me furious to die in front of him. Dexter would have died for me. He would have pressed his mask into my hands, ignorant of the consequences. They were blinking behind the smooth plastic of the face plates. I pinched the collar of my oversuit around my throat.

The sirens stopped blaring. Outside, the MPs would be testing the compound for chemicals. It occurred to me that I was going to live. I started to laugh. My aquatic friends kept huffing. I reached across the Brit's lap and took the bourbon. I thought Sedami would be offended if I drank from the bottle, so I poured the bourbon leisurely up to the meniscus line of a Dixie cup.

"*Sanguis Domini Nostri Jesu,*" I said, lifting it like a chalice to my lips. "Drink and be whole." The Dixie cup felt soft and wet. Bits of wax had separated from the side and floated in the whiskey.

I pinched a date between my gloved fingers and brought

it close to my face. I had never looked closely at a date before. I did not like the look of it, the wet brown body of an insect. I rolled over on my stomach and bit into the date while I looked at Jago. I looked at him with what I hoped was insolence and fortitude while the thick film of the date stuck to my teeth. I finished it and then I licked the tips of my gloves.

"Bear, I think I've been born again," I said.

From the klaxons on the rooftops came the call for all-clear. There was the sudden sound of breath as the others pulled their masks off their faces. Nobody said anything for a minute, and then Heppotok said, "To think I almost died without getting a kiss from Annie."

I lifted up to my knees and kissed him hard on the mouth.

"There," I said. "Now you can say you've truly lived."

My legs were shaky and I sat down hard. Sedami and Jago had begun stripping out of their oversuits. Bear picked up his banjo and leaned it against the bare wall away from us.

"Drink this," Sedami said, twisting the cap on a bottle of water.

"I'm fine," I said.

"You better go over to life support," Jago said. He was gathering his things into his helmet bag. I felt annoyed I hadn't thought of that myself. "I'll go with you," he said.

"I don't need you," I said. Jago frowned, but he kept folding his things and putting them into the bag in the right order.

"I'll take her," the Brit said. I didn't like the way he seemed to be negotiating with Jago.

"I'm fine," I repeated. I collected my gear quickly, but Jago had his bag zipped and he was waiting. There was no sense making a scene. I let him hold the door and I walked out and down the cement steps through the courtyard to the street. The moon hung crookedly over the Patriot battery on the north side of the compound. Everything was quiet. I took one step onto the road and then I threw up.

"I'm not so good," I said.

"You're too good. That's your problem."

"I didn't realize I was so drunk."

"That's the thing about being drunk. You're always the last to know."

We were crossing what was called the minefield in the middle of the compound. There were no mines in it. It was just a barren patch of dirt and rock where even the succulents wouldn't grow. There was a thin crack of blue light near the runway. Something in the back of my pack kept clinking together and I swiped at it a couple of times but couldn't get a hold of the metal.

"I'm not drunk," I said.

The heaviness of our packs made our boots sink into the sand, so that crossing the field took a long time. I walked as fast as I could. I kept stumbling on the uneven ground, but this only made me want to walk faster.

"You afraid Heppotok is going to catch up?" Jago was out of breath. He had braced his thumbs against the harness of his pack.

"Fuck Heppotok," I said.

"I'd say that's what's on his mind."

"Fuck Heppotok and fuck you."

"You're so tough, Annie."

In my room, there was nothing but a cot with a scratchy mohair blanket folded over it and my canvas bags that I'd propped against the wall. I never turned on the light when we were together but this time I did. We sat on the bed because there was no place else to sit. He put his hand on my shoulder and tried to pull me to him. It wasn't his fault, I kept thinking, it was just bad luck. But all I saw was the mask secured on his face, the four of them in their amphibious costumes, waiting for one of two things to happen.

"That's not my mouth," I said when he tried to kiss me.

"Whose mouth is it?"

"It's Pam's mouth."

"What do you want me to say, Annie? Do you want me to file for divorce from Saudi? Do you want me to make a decision right now in the middle of the war?"

"I thought you had."

"What made you think that?" He unclasped the canister from his belt and took a swig of water and offered it to me. "Have you?"

"I know what I want," I said.

"You might be disappointed, Annie. I'm lazy around the house. I have a bloodhound named Rosco who's so lazy I have to mow around him. But I like to take him out dove hunting in the fall. Ever go dove hunting, Annie? We take the pickup and go out to Lovelace Ridge near Arkansas. I use a Remington double-barrel but my buddy's got a Winchester Supreme I'd like to get my hands on. Arkansas wouldn't be a bad place to settle down, really."

"You trying to scare me?"

"I'm just saying that we have to go home sometime."

"Then why wait? If this is all so transient, why don't you go home right now?"

Then he stood up and took his pack and closed the door softly, and I wanted him to walk in again not because of what he'd told me but because he was strong enough to get up and walk out without looking back. I lay down and tried to imagine living on a ranch with a bloodhound in the backyard and wild dove carcasses in the freezer, and the scene looked comic but not impossible. I had lived in a colonial house out of something in *Yankee* magazine, and in a dilapidated saltbox in central Texas surrounded by a chicken yard, following my father into the houses of women he took up and then abandoned, so why not here, too, on a ranch in the hot American heartland? I lay there in the dark, reinventing myself, without giving a casual thought to Dexter.

But then I saw Jago sealed inside the safety of the mask. He'd done the right thing, and that irritated me. I told myself it was just bad luck that my canister had snapped, and that he had done what any soldier would do. You're a soldier first, I thought, and I tried to fill the shell of myself with the convictions of a war pilot, the confidence of someone who could walk out the door without looking back.

"Fuck Heppotok and fuck you," I said to the ceiling and fell asleep grasping the canvas ribs of the cot. But in the morning, I saw the mask over his face and then I saw our whole affair as a mask that Jago was wearing and would cast off when the war was over.

We flew that night. We went through the checklist under the red filter of the flight deck lights. The cockpit smelled of dusty and old familiar metal that had been worn down from rubbing. My headset hung over one ear so that I could hear the ground and tower and also hear Jago, in a cool and neutral voice, run through the checklist. It was as quiet and professional as if one of us was getting an eval. There was none of the usual horsing around. Even Bear stayed turned toward the INS panel, punching numbers with the efficiency of a stenographer.

On the climb out, as soon as we turned north, you could begin to see the fires popping up in Kuwait, like animals one by one opening their eyes in the night. I started a letter to my husband. *Dear Dexter*, it read, *How are things?* Jago was staring straight ahead. I crossed out the first line and wrote, *I hope everything is fine. I miss you.* Then I crossed out that line and wrote, *I've been thinking of you.*

Jago's hand was curled over the throttles, resting. I looked at his articulate knuckles and missed them, and then I turned and wrote, *You wouldn't believe what happened.*

We refueled twice and spent the long hours rooted in complacent staring. Bear didn't even play his banjo, as if waiting in protest for the easy harmony of the cockpit to resume. Just before sunrise, we listened over the radio to a Prowler and a couple of F-16s flying toward a kill box south of As Salman. Some surface-to-air missile sites in the kill box were locking up our fighters, making them jink and evade on their way to the targets, and the Prowler and Vipers had been sent to kill the missile sites. I scanned the sky for the glint of their shark-tooth bellies in the orchid smoke that hung over the desert, but the air was too thick with haze to see anything but the great boulders of soot rising from the oil fires in the east.

After a while, Jago gave me the controls and hit the aft bunks. Bear and I had a long talk about why we had joined the Air Force. I had never really talked to Bear before, and I liked him more than I thought I would. I told him how my father had been an F-86 pilot and that I had joined because of him, not that he wanted me to, but that I thought he would admire me if I did. He told me he had come in on an ROTC scholarship and that his father had been a chief master sergeant. Really, I thought, this is how things should have been throughout the war. I should never have started that whole business with Jago, and I was feeling strong and virtuous when Jago came back up to the flight deck and said, "How long have we been off course?"

The autopilot had skipped a turn point and neither of us had noticed. I had my hand resting on the throttle, and by the time I noticed that we were eighty miles north of our orbit, Jago had jumped into the left seat, brushed my hand off the throttles, and said, "My airplane."

He pushed the throttles all the way forward and pulled the yoke up hard and to the right. The Prowlers and Vipers, hunting for the surface-to-air missile, were no longer northeast but low off our nose, looking for an SA-6 that could at any moment open its eyes and launch at our broad belly, which had no business lumbering over the skies of As-Salman.

Over the radio, the Prowler called off the coordinates of a SAM whose radar had begun to scan the skies.

"Did you get those?" Jago asked Bear. "Where is it?"

I felt a sickening regret, so utter and wordless that I could not seem to reach back to a time when I had not been inept and foolhardy, and I swore that I would not speak for the rest of the war except in the line of duty and would welcome the humiliation that would come provided we only got the crew and the jet back to safety.

"Mud Six. Mud Six. Scoot 21, naked," the Prowler called over the UHF radio. The F-16s called that they were naked too, which meant the SA-6 had launched on someone else.

"Christ!" Jago yelled. We had no gear to tell us if the SAM had locked onto us or someone else. He pushed and twisted the yoke to force a quicker turn, and the jet responded as well as it could, rolling its left wing skyward and moaning into a wide, slow arc like a humpback whale.

I saw the missile come. Gray and thin as a barracuda, it flamed high into our two o'clock. Jago slammed the yoke forward. The broad, brown earth opened below us and for a moment I went blind with blood rushing into my head.

"SAM!" yelled Thumper leaning in hard and pointing over my right shoulder.

Jago banked even harder to pull the SAM across the nose and to the left side where he could see it. He called in a voice tight with the weight of gravity in his chest, "Sentry 45 engaged Mud Six."

"Sentry *who*?" called the Prowler.

We were diving hard, now. The lead F-16 launched a missile at the SAM battery. But the battery already had at least one missile in the air, and so it became a race to see whether the F-16's missile could knock out the SAM's guidance radar before their missiles killed us.

The SAM flew high and straight over.

"It's gone," I said.

"There's always two," Jago said, and as he said it, I saw the second one climbing at our one o'clock, smoke fanning out in its wake. Jago banked to the left, and the last I saw of the missile was its obliging arc, pursuing us like an urgent messenger. Then the earth skipped and floated across the windshield and we were thrown into a hurricane of sky.

I didn't know if we'd been hit dead on or just shaken by the blast of a proximity fuse. The jet seemed to twist and yaw, an unfriendly and bulbous bit of crag plummeting through the sky. The altimeter shuttered and spun. The horns and sirens began to scream. "Pull up," I yelled, though I had no idea where up was. The sun ricocheted from one part of the sky to another. The fire lights leapt out on engine three. I pulled the extinguishers without waiting for Jago's call.

"Are we still flying?" I yelled.

Even in the cockpit, the air rushing through the back of the jet was deafening. There was a puncture in the cockpit, and this led me to hope we'd been hit by the shrapnel of a proximity fuse missile and not with a full impact.

"Mission crew status," I said over net one, but I could hear nothing over the air hissing through the shattered window to my right. I pinched my nose and blew to force air into my eardrums, and then I looked at Jago. His windshield was intact. His checklist had tumbled out of his lap under the rudder pedals, and he was trying to kick it away.

I keyed the mike, but still I heard nothing. Jago put an oxygen mask over his face. His lips were moving and he looked at me, but I couldn't hear anything. He pulled on his mask to indicate I should get mine, and I reached up with my right hand and saw my comm cord had been shot clean through, and whatever it was had taken a chunk out of the hose that connected my mask to the system oxygen and caught the tip of my shoulder too. A small, dark stain of blood dribbled over the fray in my flight suit, but I felt nothing. I put my mask on, gang-loading the oxygen, and covered the rip in the hose with my right hand.

Thumper was up and leaning over my seat, flipping the forced-air switches on the overhead panel. I tapped my headset and shook my head and Jago nodded. He had his fists wrapped around the yoke, his elbows trembling with strain. By then we were at eighteen thousand in a controlled descent. The throttles were up on three of the four engines, which meant we could probably land, and I began to think that things were okay when Thumper pointed toward the grille under Bear's feet. The radios in the lower lobe were golden with fire.

"They down there?" I yelled to Thumper, and he nodded, meaning the fire team had gone through the aft grille. There was no way to know if anyone in back was hurt. As we descended, the entrails of the ground smoke began to lap at the side of the fuselage. We were descending into Saudi Arabia toward what I assumed was King Kaleed airstrip. I looked back at Bear. He'd taken his gloves off and he was zipping his banjo into its soft vinyl case. I poked him on the arm and held my hand up to show that he should put his gloves on, but he shook his head and kept working the zipper around the rim.

I reset the alarms to silence them. In spite of the air whistling through the cracked windshield, the cockpit became hazy with smoke. In the narrow corridor behind the cockpit, the two firefighters crawled back through the open grille next to the first row of consoles. They made a sign that the fire was out but that the wires were smoldering. Jago pointed toward the flap indicators and cocked his hands in opposite directions to show that we had asymmetric flaps.

I nodded, and then I sat dumbly in the copilot's seat. If he'd told me we had only one wing, or that the back half of the jet was gone, or that we'd just set the whole war effort back six months, I would not have been surprised. I assumed this would be my last flight, that I'd either die or be stripped of my wings and court-martialed. I saw myself standing at the center of gray, austere rooms, dressed in Class-As before councils of senior officers, reading formal apologies while right and rank were stripped one by one like so many insignia from my uniform, and what shamed me the most was not enduring that ritual but the moment when I would stand in civilian clothes facing Jago, who would never have fallen upon his own mask, never let the course of an aircraft slip out of his hands. He would regard me as all pilots do when they see comrades fall from their station, with pity and loathing, as the strong regard the weak.

The airstrip was broadening. We were crabbing at forty-five degrees and running too fast. None of this scared me. Fear of death is a sharp, heart-pounding jolt, but what I felt was the cold, heavy bladder of dread. I longed vaguely to get everyone out of the jet. I prayed for the crew, though my prayers had nothing to do with faith. They were just pleas of desperation, the kind you make as a child when either wonderful or horrible things loom out of your control.

At five thousand, the smoke was as thick as vapor inside the cockpit.

"We're overshooting," I said. The lights from the crash trucks flashed along the runway.

"Gear!"

I pulled the gear handle, and we got two green lights on the main gear. I didn't have to call it. Jago was staring at the lights and I saw his lips move next to the mike and knew he was calling tower to ask if our nose gear had come down also. Then he shook his head at me and I knew we were going in anyway and that Jago would try to keep us rolling on the main gear as long as possible and edge us down gently on the nose.

Even with bad flaps, he kept us straight on the runway, and I thought about how good he was, how instinctual and calm, and how he would save the crew from my recklessness. We rolled past the off-ramps, past the crash trucks and fire engines. The nose remained high as though resisting the day's final affront. Jago gave a last push on the yoke and the nose tumbled down, jolting us forward and slamming Thumper into the back of my seat. We kept sliding, so close to the ground that I could see the speckles in the paving and the variations in the skid marks.

We skidded like a derby car off the end of the runway into the dust. Jago hit the evacuation bell.

"Out," he said. "Out now. Bear, I want you to—"

Bear was tucked under the nav console working the banjo free. It had gotten wedged between the bulkhead and Jago's seat.

"Leave it!" Jago screamed.

"Fuck you," Bear yelled.

"Forget the fucking banjo."

The radios in the lobe under us had caught fire again. Smoke bubbled through the grille in the floor. Jago slapped at the breakers over our heads.

"Get out!" he yelled at me. Thumper was half-squatting on the floor with his arms thrown over the throttles.

"He's hurt," I yelled.

"Get him out of here."

"I can't move my arm," I said. "You have to help him." He looked at me and the logic of the solution registered, and he seemed to resent me for it. "I got it," I said. "I'll shut down. Go."

Jago climbed over the throttles and pulled Thumper's arm over his shoulder. Thumper was breathing hard and clutching his ribs, and they shuffled out of the cockpit toward the forward port door where the radio operator had already pulled the slide handle.

I looped the oxygen hose over my seat where I could stand at Thumper's console and slap at the breakers with my good hand. I couldn't close my right hand over the gash in the hose now, and a pungent smoke began to slip in with the oxygen, but I had to make sure the engines and electricity were shut down so that there was no explosion in the few minutes it would take the crew to egress. Bear pulled himself up from the floor and knelt on Jago's seat, his feet flopped over the throttles, trying to work the banjo out of the niche between the bulkhead and the seat rails. I was still hitting the breakers, and I pulled my leg up and kicked him hard in the ass. That only made him jerk more frantically at the instrument. His broad backside jiggled between the yoke and the chair back and I kicked the soft flesh over and over until he straightened up, his red face huffing under the mask, and said, "Let me be!"

"Don't be stupid!" I yelled. My voice echoed inside the auditorium of my mask. I had the urge to smash the banjo to pieces, stomp out the possibility of rescue but also the lunatic desire that kept Bear lingering over the kind of death that would seem pathetic and suicidal, full of bad judgment, and one that even Bear, in a saner moment, would see as indulgent and embarrassing.

"I can't tell where it's hung up." His face was scarlet. He blinked, his eyes tearing in the smoke. I could see the brightness of the windshield and imagined, well beyond the nose, the crew assembling for the head count and the medics working over the injured. My hair was damp with sweat and I felt a burning in my eyes and the edges of my ears and in my right shoulder where the blood had seeped into the green nomex along my arm. I began to cough with the acrid fumes in my throat. It felt as though the cockpit had closed up around us, as though we'd stumbled into a treacherous ocean cave, and now in the thickening smoke, Bear seemed to be moving away from me, deeper into the cockpit whose shapes and instruments no longer felt familiar but like sinister, startling hazards.

"Do you want to die here?" I shouted. "Is a banjo worth dying over?" He didn't answer me, but in a sense he did, because if you have to hesitate after that kind of question, the answer is already clear.

"It's my fault," I yelled. "Hate me, but do it outside." We both sucked twice on the oxygen and let the masks slide over our heads and onto the seats. I followed him through the cockpit to the portside door where the sun burnt a halo in the hazy smoke floating in the dark aft of the airplane. The radios in the forward lobe hissed under the grilles. Punctures like buckshot holes pierced the starboard side of the fuselage. Some of the insulation and panels had fallen down, but the heavy cabinets were intact and the jet looked like the dark, empty hull of a dying whale.

Outside, the firefighters had begun to spray the jet with foam. Bear leapt first, launching himself almost halfway down the slide where he bounced and tumbled to the bottom. I braced my right arm and jumped, sliding into the brightness that burned through the sweat in my eyes. Then I was up and running toward the voices calling our names.

Jago caught me. I bent down and spit black mucus on the ground.

"What took you so long?"

"Bear—," I began, but I couldn't breathe with running and the images of the cockpit that now seemed surreal and indescribable.

"Medic!" Jago yelled.

"Medic? Nobody ever yells 'Medic.'"

"Stay here," he said. In the moment he was gone, I noticed the circus of flashing lights parked well away from the edge of the runway where our jet lilted like a parched, frothing bird with its nose in the dust. Three of our operators lay on stretchers attended by clusters of medics and officers from the squadron.

Jago returned with a thick pad of white gauze folded in his hand.

"How is everybody?" I said.

"Everyone's fine."

"Thumper?"

"Cracked ribs, that's all."

"Nobody dead?"

He shook his head. He tried to put the bandage up to my arm, but I shook him off. "I want to know," I said.

"Everyone's fine," he said again. "Lancey broke his wrist. Grady bent his knee up pretty bad. Just you and Bear were—what took you so long?"

"We were goddamn lucky," I said. The other crew members, ones with lesser injuries, sat in the shade of the emergency trucks holding cloths or ice packs to their faces and legs or stood staring at the jet.

"It wasn't your fault. Not entirely," he said. "The E-3 skips turn points all the time."

"Save it," I said. "I'm ready for it, as long as the crew is okay."

"We'll all testify," he said. "They should have seen it in the backend, that the jet was off-course."

He was still holding the cloth in his hand. I took it from him and pressed it to my shoulder, and then I said, "I wouldn't have done it, either. Given up my mask. If things were reversed, I would have done what you did."

Jago looked down at the ground for a moment. "It shouldn't have gone like that. I don't want to remember that mask as the last thing between us."

I shrugged. "The result would have been the same when we got home, only it would have taken me longer to understand."

There was nothing else to say. The blunt steel feeling of dread was gone. I would lose Jago, and I would lose my wings, but the crew was safe and I welcomed the punishment that would come. It would be the first time I would stand up as myself, not hidden behind the armor of my wings, and I was ready for that.

My wound began to sting under the hot morning sun. I walked over and sat in the shade of one of the fire trucks. Thumper and two of the other crew had already been lifted on stretchers into the ambulance. A young-looking medic with strawberry hair squatted over me and began to clean my shoulder, and it burned down to the bone.

"Nasty scratch," he said. "You'll be able to show your kids a battle scar."

"I don't have kids."

He smiled. "Well, you've got time."

The jet sat limply with its chin buried in the dust. Bear stood off its nose, so close that a fireman had to keep waving him off. I sat watching him and yearning for Jago, the freshness of a love affair whose only consequence was the daily uncertainty of battle and the innocence of never wanting more.

# PART III

# Into the Fluid Air

# 7.

"IT'S LIKE A WEDDING, ALL THE DRESSING AND PICTURE taking, marching up and down the aisles. I wonder if nuns feel like this when they're consecrated. Is consecrate what you do with nuns?"

"Only when they turn to stone." Dexter tugged at the lapel of my Class-As. "When's the last time you wore this, fifth grade?" We were standing in the parking lot outside the wing auditorium, Dexter working intricately at my jacket, straightening the medal under the deck of ribbons on my chest. I could feel his hand pulling the fabric taut. It was like the numbness of a local anesthetic under a surgeon's knife.

"This doesn't fit."

"It never did. What did your mother give me? It wasn't Tylenol."

"God knows." He fastened the pin, leaned back to view the results.

"I can't believe I'm going through with this."

"You don't have to believe it. You just have to do it."

"That's better than what they used to say. They used to say I had to believe, too."

"So it's better this way?" He unhooked the pin on the medal, a Distinguished Flying Cross, and moved it again. Around us, the cars were thinning out of the parking lot. Dexter's parents and my father and Hannah had already left for the celebration dinner at the Petroleum Club.

"No. I can't imagine it being any worse."

"I can." He cocked his head, focused, breathing between parted lips. "There, now you're presentable."

"How could it be worse?" He'd circled around and was sliding the jacket off my shoulders.

"The thing about you, Annie, the thing that gets to me"— he was tugging at the collar of my blouse where a clotted stitch had left the seam not quite perfect—"is that you just don't see what's right in front of you."

"Is this about you? Does every issue have to be about you?"

"You don't get it, Annie. Look at me."

"I can't do this right now. I don't want to do this. Look, let's go."

"It's not as big as it seems right now. When you look at the future, this whole thing doesn't matter that much."

"Let's drop it. How did we get here?" I asked.

"Believing. We were talking about whether it's better or worse."

Dexter lay the jacket in the trunk of the car with the sleeves folded over the pockets. It lay stolid, like a corpse in a funeral procession.

"Believing is better," I said. "But it doesn't last. Can I have the keys?"

"Should you be driving?"

"I'm fine, just relaxed. Besides, driving gives me the illusion that I have some kind of control over my life."

We had Dexter's father's Mercedes. His parents had gone with my father and Hannah in the Lincoln. Dexter's father, Wayne, had said riding in the Lincoln was better than riding in a Chinook over Musan. My father had said it was better than cruising in an F-80 over the Yalu. All day they were one-upping each other with war stories and flying stories and stories of bravado, Wayne initiating with hopeful, eager glances at my father, and my father responding with clips of anecdotes, cast off with casual bravado, that left you sensing a richer story veiled in modesty, or perhaps decency.

This style was, I knew, designed for the two women (excluding me) in the audience and had the usual effect. Hannah listened in adoration. June watched him with repose, but her eyes glimmered, her lips compressed, trembling at the corners. He told the kind of stories that never quite ended. In 1946, he'd worked on a banana boat with the Merchant Marines and couldn't touch bananas for years afterward. In 1951, he'd driven repeatedly around the Tower of Pisa in a Jeep, trying to figure out which way it was leaning. In 1958, he'd flown into the eye of a hurricane. All his stories involved movement, and that was enough for women like Hannah and June to believe they were going somewhere, that they could evoke some larger meaning. I should count myself among women like Hannah and June. I listened to the stories, too. I let them go to work on my imagination, even as I knew that, if pressed, the story's ending would never quite arrive, that any point or lesson or implication was one of my own making.

There was a new element to the telling. His voice, with its pleasant Southern sound, was even softer now with the cancer in his lungs, wavering, sometimes rasping at the edge of that precipice we could all sense but could hardly envision. He was immortal. I thought I'd caught up to him, but he'd eluded me again, achieved a state of detachment and reverence that I could either envy or despise, but not attain.

We went out the back gate and down the narrow road to the interstate. The road was quiet and badly patched and the sparseness of the land was concealed behind the tall grass and clusters of oaks at its edge.

*Dear Dad,*

*What you've been reading is a mockery of everything I have believed. The events are not as they appear in the news, not as heroic, not as clear-sighted. Please do us both the favor of not attending the award ceremony. Avoid the newspaper articles. Preserve, in your abstinence, the higher existence I'd hoped to achieve.*

\*　　　\*　　　\*

"I should have sent the letter," I said.

"What letter? What are you talking about?"

"It doesn't matter. Wouldn't you like to read all the letters that are written and never sent? I bet they're better than the ones that make it."

"Are you okay?"

"The trees are bothering me a little. I wish they would slow down."

"Why don't you let me drive."

"Don't be silly. I'm a pilot. It's just that the trees are bothering me."

"You're scaring me, Annie. This isn't safe."

"Safe? I'm the courier of safe. I'm safe's angel. Nothing can touch you under my wings."

"Please pull over."

"We're almost there. Please take your hand off the wheel."

"Do you see the light?"

"Of course I see the light. The light of reason. The light of beauty. The light of the oncoming train."

"The red light. I mean the red light."

I made a point of slowing smoothly, so smoothly that the difference between motion and stillness was imperceptible.

"You see?"

"What are you trying to prove to me? I'm the last person you have to prove something to."

"And then there's everybody else."

"So you finally get to be a martyr, what you've always wanted to be."

"That's funny, Dex. I'm glad you're enjoying this."

"I am. Except for the driving, I really am."

They were waiting for us when we arrived. The Petroleum Club was Wayne's idea. This was one place he could one-up my father with no contention. We walked in, under the triumphant archway, past the fountain of water glittering over the gilded tiles, to the elevator that would transport us to that remote, ethereal place: the executive dining room, which Wayne presented to my father like a Napoleonic gift. My father, ever the fighter pilot, scanned the room with his cool, approving gaze, but it was Hannah who exclaimed, "Oh, Wayne, it's just like Versailles!"

The maître d' escorted our little procession through the gathering of early diners, some of whom lifted their gazes from their delicate-looking canapés to nod at me with looks of appreciation. A few said, "Congratulations," and "Nice job, Captain." I tried to respond with a nod to each of them until I realized I must look like a chicken pecking at seed.

Wayne and my father spent several minutes deferring the table's head to each other, and then at last Wayne held the chair for my father, insisting upon the honor, and my father consented, moving slowly, eminently, toward the table's prow while the rest of us settled into the flanking seats.

My father, thin as I'd ever seen him, sat across from Hannah, the hollows of his face softened in the glow of ivory linens and candlelight. He'd taken his sand-colored Desert Storm cap off for the occasion. A few wisps of white hair clung resolutely to his pink scalp. He'd always appeared undaunted in crowds, but there was now, in addition, a sort of nobility, as though he'd not merely submitted to the nearness of death but had made a truce with it. He was weak but not in pain. He ate enormously, yet weight fell off his body. His mind was sound, sad, guilty, and balanced with such composure that he seemed gigantic as ever. In comparison to his, *my* life, *my* war, *my* wound, felt histrionic and trivial.

Wayne ordered champagne. Next to him, June lifted her head slightly, scanning the room for known faces, measuring its regal weight. She'd wanted us to celebrate in Houston, at *their* Petroleum Club, and then spend the weekend at their ranch, but there was the concern of my father spending another day stretched in the front seat of the Lincoln under the sway of Hannah's driving. Dexter had suggested the club in Oklahoma City, and June acquiesced, reserving rooms at the Ambassador. Dexter had taken every new development with glee, having finally overcome the astonishment of the press interviews, the news articles, the one home video clip of Bear and me sliding down the chute that played over and over in the news. He wanted to be interviewed as the husband of the first woman to receive the DFC, but the only newspaper offered was the *Washington Times*, which was looking for an angle on how the rise of professional military women was eroding home values. He declined.

"Why?" I'd asked him. "Why end the hubris there?"

"And hold my wife back? You're a genuine hero. Well, not *genuine*. But you know what I mean. You're on the fast track. It would be so tacky to contradict you. It would be so, what's the word, *gauche.*"

"You're in rare form today, Dexter. I wish you would do the *Standard* interview. Then we could do the talk-show circuit, the heroine pilot and her conservative, God-fearing— you're going to have to start fearing God—husband. And then we can write a book and retire in Costa Rica. We can run a bar there. You can invent a drink called Annie's Flying Cross."

"It's got potential," he said.

I'd told Dexter everything as it happened, beginning with the investigation board, the contents of the report that was later "sealed," the meeting Jago and I had with the wing commander, how we had sat in his office crafting the words of the DFCs we would both receive, how the press had pushed Jago aside clamoring to interview me. I told Dexter everything except why I'd let the jet drift over an SA-6 site in the first place and why Jago and I hardly spoke a word to each other during the whole ordeal.

At the Petroleum Club, Dexter made the first toast of the evening, something about virtues born of impudence, vices fathered by heroism. Nobody followed it, but nobody had to. They were all sold on the evening, the serene graciousness of the weeping chandeliers, the cummerbunded wait staff, the pale, pensive walls that whispered of brocade, that comprehended the misfortune of foreign wars, their necessary evils, and silently dismissed them. Wayne and my father seized the remaining toasts, offering them to each other and to the wars of the past. There was a sense that they were toasting, too, the wars of the future, the soldiers not yet initiated into our lucky tribe.

"Well, I didn't earn any Silver Star," Wayne said, referring to the medal my father had earned in Korea. Wayne had been a radioman with the Army. "All I remember is the cold. Damn, it was cold."

"It was so cold the latrines used to freeze."

"It was so cold my toes were blue for six months."

"They used to say to sleep with your clothes off, that it would keep you warmer. I tried it both ways, clothes on and clothes off, and I never could tell which way was best." My father gave a little laugh and lifted the handkerchief to his nose.

"It's only clothes off if you're with somebody else," I said. My head had begun to hurt again, not in a precise way, not in any place I could pinpoint, just a general, steady throbbing, with a muffled noise like the beating of a base drum covered in raw bacon. "June, have you got another Tylenol? That's what they teach you in survival. To avoid hypothermia."

I expected a look of admonishment, a flicker of the warning of older days, when a misbehavior might invite consequences, but instead my father winced slightly, as though he'd been gripped with a twinge of pain.

"Korea was unusual," Wayne said. "They don't fight wars that way anymore."

"Everybody forgot about Korea," my father said.

"Oh, everybody's going to forget about the Gulf War, too," I said. "The shortest war in history. Is that all the champagne?"

"Well, actually, there was the Six Days War," Hannah said. "I remember that from my Awakening to the Middle East extension class."

"And Grenada," Dexter said.

"Okay," I said. "A bit of trivia. The shortest war in history happened a hundred years ago. England and Zanzibar. Lawrence and the Arabian Nights. The sultan had a hundred wives, and he slept with five a night, starting a new cycle every twenty days."

"Like the moon," Hannah said.

"Almost," my father said.

"There was some scuttle with England after the sultan died—of a heart attack, probably—and the English took the castle in forty-five minutes. Must have surprised them more than anybody."

"Bravo, Annie," Dexter said.

"You must be tired." June caressed the stem on her champagne glass.

"She's been decorated." Hannah winked, her fork poised over the endive salad.

"Like a tree," I said.

"What really happened out there, Annie?" Hannah asked. "I've been dying to know."

My father had told me once, in an unguarded moment, that the best pilots never tell war stories. They might suggest, imply, defer to the imagination, but to actually tell a story was crass. He wasn't being entirely truthful. There were nights when, as a little girl, I sat hidden in a corner between the buffet and the window, ankles tucked under my nightgown, listening to the stories growing more outrageous as the night grew long. These were stories told among pilots at a certain time of night, when the women were all in some other corner of the house, and the children were quiet, and certain of the stories could be brought out, like swords unsheathed, and handed around and admired.

"It's terribly long, and most of it is classified."

"Oh, of course, but there must be parts—I mean, we've read about it."

"I was disoriented. I hardly remember anything."

"Annie's being modest," Hannah said. "She's so terribly modest."

"It's all right here," my father said. "It's all in print, every word as it happened."

My father unfolded the citation from somewhere in the cavernous flap of his jacket—he was so thin—and unfolded it with a tremor in his fingertips.

"'Attention to order,'" he read, his voice wavering yet steadfast, a flag streaming gallantly over the ramparts, "'Citation to accompany the Distinguished Flying Cross is awarded to Captain Annie Viola Shaw for singularly distinctive valor in the face of the enemy.'"

"Viola?" June whispered.

"Her grandmother's name," Dexter said.

"'On February first, 1991, Captain Shaw piloted her crippled aircraft safely after taking enemy fire and being wounded by a surface-to-air missile through skilled airmanship and extreme personal courage.'"

"Yes," I said. "I was certainly wounded through airmanship, skilled or not."

"'Captain Shaw fought through severed communications and wounds to her head and shoulders to bring the aircraft safely back to friendly territory, executing an emergency landing with one engine down and a dysfunctional nose gear.'"

"Ha. If you thought the nose gear was dysfunctional, you should have seen the pilot."

" 'When the aircraft came to a stop, Captain Shaw risked her own life to ensure the crew egressed safely while shutting the remaining aircraft systems down, preventing further injury to her crew.' "

"Thank God I didn't cause them any further injury."

" 'She personally evacuated the navigator who was temporarily incapacitated.' "

"Incapacitated. That was the wing commander's idea."

" 'The singularly distinctive accomplishments of Captain Shaw reflect great credit upon herself and the United States Air Force.' "

My father paused, scanning the words once again as if to confirm their validity. Dexter nodded slightly, with not the slightest spark of light in his eyes.

"That's just beautiful," Hannah said. "Read it again."

I suppose the only thing that saved me from a full investigation was the end of the war. Who could have the heart to punish us in the face of all that victory, even if we had been the last airborne casualty? Simply put, Lieutenant Colonel Sprecht could. The deputy squadron commander, who'd spent the war signing safety evaluations at Tinker Air Force Base, took relish in pursuing the court-martial of Jago and me. He even tried to work Killer, the surveillance officer, into the equation, though Killer was sick and grounded on that particular flight.

The investigation board was waiting for us when we returned, and Spacely stood at its broad and condemning helm. I could feel the judgment in the room, had felt it before countless times in officer training and pilot training. Being a woman in the military seemed to invite appraisal, though not this time. They focused on Jago because he was the aircraft commander. That was the worst part. He had to answer for my mistakes. And he took the heat. Perhaps *that* was the worst part. He accepted the blame for my shortcomings, as a parent accepts blame for a child's delinquency. I don't think we'd looked at each other directly since that moment outside the burning jet, and perhaps *that* was the worst part, to be implicated with him and yet so far removed. There was a list of worst parts, and I recounted them now in my head, searching for recompense.

"All this attention is hard, isn't it?" Wayne leaned over the roast tenderloin, freshly served, to whisper to me. "It's like serving duty all over again."

Spacely didn't realize there were larger forces at work. Someone had got a copy of the video clip to the news networks, and on the day that the board convened, the press were showing the clip repeatedly on the nightly news, at regular speed and in slow motion, beginning with the moment Bear appeared in the doorway, looking dazed by the brightness and surprised at the action on the ground in front of him. He draws back for a moment, but perhaps this is only to get momentum for the jump, which he executes, landing nearly halfway down the slide and bouncing the rest of the way down. Two firemen run toward him, lift him to his feet and pull him away. I don't hesitate at all. I stumble out of the doorway—perhaps I've tripped on the matting that covers the portal to the lower lobe—and land on my elbows and knees, somersaulting down the slide and hitting the ground on my feet like a perfectly executed stunt. Then I am up and running and someone is running toward me and I fall into him so that he stumbles backward catching me. This is Jago, of course. I don't remember falling into him. He puts his hand behind my head, yells something over his shoulder, and now I am grasping his collar, burying my head in his chest. It's an intimate moment, one Dexter must have noticed. The press made everything they could of this clip—they were starved for news—and by the end of the week, the wing commander had received so many calls that the investigation board was dismissed and Jago and I were instructed on how all the questions would be answered.

"We're proud of your trimmings," Dexter said.

"Why are you doing this to me?" I whispered to him.

"Because martyrdom suits you," he whispered back. "It's your dream come true."

"I don't believe I've heard the story of how you earned your medal," June said to my father.

Sometimes all the forces in the world come together, just for a moment, reverberating in a single, harmonious hum as though to remind us that there is some sense to the world. June had just casually asked a question I'd spent my whole childhood edging around, not daring to ask, never expecting an answer, and my father was looking at her now, contemplating a response.

"I didn't earn it," he said. "I have it, but I didn't earn it."

"What does that mean?" I asked.

"That's all it means," he said. "That's the most important part."

"Did you fly in Korea, or is that a misunderstanding, too?"

He looked at me quickly and then raised his chin, as though I'd slapped him, and answered, "More than I care to remember."

I looked away. The waiters were working noiselessly in the room. I imagined, with pleasure, two of them colliding, scattering chateaubriand and potatoes bedded in rosehips all over the pearl-colored carpet. What could you say to a man who was your father, and was dying, and had stolen every moment of your life and somehow made you look like the thief?

"I was just wondering which illusions you created and which ones I came up with myself."

"I never told you any stories that weren't true."

"That's because you never told me any stories."

"And would you like to hear this one? Would it help you?"

"It might have helped me. It might have helped me understand you."

"You didn't need to understand me when you were young. You needed to believe in me. You lost your mother. You needed a hero. I'd like to think that's helped shape who you are."

"Oh, it has," I said.

Hannah's eyes were shining. June's lips were quivering. "You were trying to be a good provider," one of them, perhaps June, said. Dexter had taken my hand, and his thumb was caressing the knobs of my knuckles, trying perhaps to get me to loosen them, to reach in return for him.

"It wasn't easy for me, either," he said. "You can't admit your mistakes when you're young. It's too painful. You have to keep telling yourself you did the right thing, whatever it was, just to get by."

He paused now, leaning back in the chair, and the breathing rose visibly in his chest. "I used to think that character was something you built on, but I think it's different now. I think life is like an onion skin, and you peel it back to the essentials of who you are."

"Why didn't you tell me this a long time ago?" I asked.

"You're luckier than you realize," he said. "You're lucky you don't have to carry the burden of false heroism. I wouldn't wish that on anyone."

I might have laughed. I might have given up the whole thing right there. I think I even smiled. My father looked at me. There was pain in his eyes, real pain, and I thought it must come from never knowing if you've made the right decisions or from, as my father used to say, never recognizing the big mistakes until it was too late.

"You're father's an amazing man," Hannah said, but she wasn't looking at me.

After dinner, as we stood in the atrium waiting for the adults—we would always, until we had our own children, be the children—Dexter asked again if I was all right. In the mirror behind a great vase of tulips, I noticed some strands of hair had come unpinned and lay across my shoulders. I lifted my arms to fix them and felt the sleeves nearly bursting. The last time I'd worn the uniform I was graduating from pilot training. We'd stood in the sun for an hour while the speeches and flag ceremonies rolled on. The shoes were just as uncomfortable then, two-and-a-half-inch heels in black patent leather I'd bought that morning in a panic after realizing my own shoes were too cheap to wear to a ceremony. I'd been just as anxious that afternoon to get the uniform off, get into some jeans and have a drink, all the formality behind me. In another week, I'd be on my way to Tinker for training with AWACS.

"I'm going to resign," I said.

"Okay."

"I want to move. Let's go someplace else."

"Okay."

"You know, my father did tell me a story once. He told me that when I was eight years old, he had an attack of pancreatitis while he was alone at home. We must have been between women then. He said he'd made it to the phone to call an ambulance—I guess you just dialed the operator in those days—and he collapsed. He told me he left his body and he was floating up toward something light and warm, and that he wanted to go there, but he knew I'd be home from school soon and he didn't want me to find him like that, so he came back. He came back to his body for me. He said he didn't mind being back in his body because he knew home was out there where the light was. I always thought that was a wonderful story. What do you think? Is it a good story?"

"No," Dexter said. "It's a horrible story."

Then he took me in his arms and I started to cry.

# 8.

WE LIVE ON A RANCH NOW, WHAT WE CALL A RANCH, IN what Dexter calls the foothills of San Antonio. In fact, the structure is a chunky ingot-like rectangular slab of granite intended to house servants as part of an elaborate design that was never completed. The limestone casing is a lovely textured peach-and-rose-colored stone that intimates how splendid the main manse would have been had the owner not died of a heart attack while the land on the plateau across the stream was cleared and readied, and had his widow not abandoned the project, selling the entire two hundred and ten acres to us on very good terms. The ranch is quite dark, which is a blessing in the summer heat, because of the way it was positioned to afford privacy to the main residence. No doors lead out to the main part of the property, which begins as a garden of giant oaks descending toward the stream, and it can only be viewed from the high, squat windows on the eastern side. There is a screened-in cement patio on the western side, facing a field of king-ranch bluestem and a cluster of elms that shroud the road. Here is where we sit most evenings, in the ebbing heat, just as the servants would have sat, oriented toward the road. A bluff called Mother's Mountain breaks the horizontal landscape, and this is where the sun buries its nose at dusk. The king-ranch bluestem, an immigrant pest that chokes native plants, gives off in spite of itself a pleasant violet glow. If we are quiet enough, the deer jump the wire fence to eat at the corn feeder Dexter built in the front yard. These few moments, before darkness claims the field, are what I've come to see as the kernel of my life, the inexorable calm that comes with the passage into night. Days are the hard part. Days, I'm still learning to love.

Dexter, by contrast, is a morning person, and this morning, as always, he is up before the cotton spiders have removed their webs. He starts the coffee brewing and tiptoes through the narrow French doors out to the patio to read the paper and commune with his deer. He's been told not to feed the deer corn—it destroys their intestines—but he does it anyway. I usually take a book out—at the moment it's a culinary textbook, because I'm determined to learn how to cook—and flip the pages as quietly as I can. The deer feed like prey, lifting their heads every few minutes to investigate their situation. We're overrun with them in southern Texas. They're like the kangaroo in Australia, or the black bears in Washington, a dazzling manifestation of nature that becomes mundane, and then a nuisance. We lease out the back hundred and sixty acres for hunting. I've suggested to Dexter that it's wrong to feed the deer and then hunt them, but he says it's all right as long as we only hunt them on the back lot, behind the stream, as though the deer know the difference.

"You about ready?" he asks.

Mornings, if Dexter is not offsite at a rig, we go out walking in the grass. He folds his paper, rinses his cup, and places it on the rubber mat at the sink's edge—one of a hundred little habits that amuse me. You would think we were an old couple, long in marriage, whose silences belie a subtle, continuous conversation. We are not this kind of couple. In our silence there is only silence, and this is the hardest part of the day to bear.

I wear nylon pants and walk behind him. The land here is dry and desperate, and every living thing gets along by sticking, stinging, and biting anything it can. These walks began as exercise and have become little adventure trips. We collect, in a cardboard box on the patio, artifacts we find buried in the paths and limestone beds, flint arrowheads and tiny fossils, some so perfectly preserved that they might have been discarded, or petrified, the previous day. "Look," he says happily, as though we are on a sort of Easter egg hunt of the natural world. Yesterday we came upon a skunk stalking grasshoppers. We were only ten or so feet from it—too close—and Dexter held his hand up as a sign to be still. We stood so long in silence except for the rustling of the skunk's claws in the grass that I began to believe that this might be enough—that this was *something*—to be furtive witness to a skunk's unguarded moment.

"Are *you* ready?" I ask, because today we've planned more than an ordinary walk. We have an airplane, a Cessna 172, and a runway on the back one-sixty, and I've been teaching Dexter to fly. Today is his first solo. He breaks into a grin. He's been eager for this, and I try to be excited, too. I try to believe he is doing this for himself and not to please or impress me.

We start as everyday, crossing around to the back and under the array of grand oaks—God's Garden, Dexter once called it, which startled me. He is typically neither metaphoric nor spiritual, and I frowned at him because the term was so perfect and so casually stated, and it made me suspect I have not really listened to Dexter and that he may not be the person I've decided he is. Of course, I have *not* been listening to him, and part of me does not want to know what I've been missing. Then we walk down the hill and across the stream, which flows out of a spring where I often go at lunchtime with a book and a lawn chair and sit with my ankles dangling in the water, reading good, rich stories, consuming them like truffles one on top of another. I'm jealous of these writers—the lives they lead and portray—and I believe that I could have the same experiences, the same feelings, in my own life if I didn't isolate myself here, with Dexter, on this ranch so far from the highway.

But I believe this everywhere I go. I believed it when I was flying in the middle of a war, that at the end of it, I could leave with Jago and fly off into paradise. I picture us saying goodbye to everyone, lifting into the fluid air, moving toward the promise of some vague destination. We would have ended up in a place not so different than this. My life would have been much the same. Inevitably, I would have begun to want something beyond my grasp, with Jago just one more dream conquered. I know that, and yet I yearn for it.

The plateau on the other side of the stream is thick with tall grass and raspy cedar. Fire ants build soft tufts of dirt everywhere. On the other side of the plateau, as you turn east away from the road, is another riverbed, but this one is dry. The pale, round rocks in it look dry and ancient: dinosaurian. Here Dexter stops to search for fossils, and he's good at finding them. He can guess their age and name the period and tell me what was going on then. I'm intimidated by his expertise, perplexed by his contentment to scratch and sniff around in the riverbeds for evidence of evolutionary progress. It's as though I ask every morning how I got here, how I wound up at this ranch that fits me like the inherited cloak of a grande dame, and Dexter seems to reply, "It all started with this shell."

He dusts the dry bed with his fingers, works out a gastropod that is white and chalky, a fossilized snail the size of a baseball.

"Glen Rose formation?"

"Probably. Certainly Cretaceous. So why did you tell Caroline we're going to Mexico next weekend?"

"Because I don't want to visit her. I don't want to go back there." Maybe the house has changed, or maybe it's exactly the same, but either way, I don't want to go inside or even see it. Justin is gone, of course, long grown and married with his own family in Galveston, but there's something else, some faint hope or promise inside that house I can't bear to remember.

"You can't put her off forever."

"Yes, I can. She's a Southern lady. She'll get the hint."

Last evening, we walked this path with Caroline Biddix. She drives down in her Grand Cherokee every couple of months. She has short, crimpy hair that looks like an untwilled rope and she wears jeans and carries the faint smell of figs. Her parents have long since passed away and she lives alone. I know I should visit her, but I can't bring myself to walk up the steps of the sloping porch and into the parlor with the Hammond organ and confront a hundred details now mercifully sifted from memory. Instead, I tell myself that she likes the drive. She likes to come out to the riverbed in the evenings and hunt for arrowheads, and she's found several. She looks at them every time she visits, but she won't take any home.

"They belong here," she said last night, "like you."

"Me?"

"This place needed you, and you needed it."

We were sitting on the patio eating grilled steak on the bright Mexican plates we bought last year in Laredo.

"It's growing on me," I said. "If I wait long enough, it will grow *over* me."

"Annie's never happy unless she's dissatisfied," Dexter said. "She hardly eats anymore, so I guess she must love it here."

"I can think of worse places," Caroline said. "Do you

know, there was a woman out here some years ago who was buried sitting behind the wheel of her powder blue Ferrari."

"Buried as in *dead* and buried?" I asked.

Caroline nodded. "An oil heiress. She was wearing silk lingerie. It was quite a funeral. Made the papers all over the state."

"Don't give Annie ideas. She'll want to be buried in the Cessna."

"Don't bury me. Just leave me in the hangar wearing goggles and a bomber jacket. That'll be much more dramatic."

"You could have a military funeral like your father did," Caroline said.

"I don't think so."

"But you were a war hero," she said. "You could be buried at Arlington."

"No, I wasn't," I said.

"You and your father, both."

"My father was an operator, that's all. He was good, but he was an operator. It took me a long time to understand that."

If Caroline was hurt, she didn't show it. But later, after she left, Dexter said, "That was cruel."

"It was honest," I said. "What's wrong with honesty?"

"She's a lonely lady who wants to remember her one true love in a good light. Let her have that."

"Why do they always remember my father as their one true love? You know who his true love was?"

"Not you."

"Very good, Dex. Maybe if she realized that, too, she could move on."

"Like you have?"

"Yes, like I have."

We lay in bed last night in silence, under the swirling fan, and again I didn't tell him why I have no appetite and what is taking root in my body.

ABOVE THE riverbed, we cross into the back one-sixty, where the runway is. It was an auxiliary runway for a World War II training base called Whirley Field, where the Pacific Air School conducted training on the PT-17 biplane, according to documents in the local library. What the library could not reveal was why we found some rusty 50-caliber shells on the hunting grounds behind the runway, and it pleases me to imagine the land was secretly used for targeting practice in the years before Korea.

We inherited a single twenty-two-hundred-foot runway, eroded and pocked, which we've since repaved, and the remains of an old hangar, stripped of its rolling doors, where we keep the Cessna we purchased as a "business asset" for Dexter's surveying trips. In reality, I use it for pleasure flying, and in the spring I flew two Mexican brothers—exchange students, or wetbacks, they're called here—up to work on our land and on the land of one of Dexter's cousins. I flew low to avoid being picked up by the aerostats, and it gave me great pleasure to put some of my military knowledge to use. In another life, I would have been horrified at what amounts to slave labor, but there's a natural economy here, near the border, that lives in the gap between poverty and the working class. I never understood the term *wetback*. At first I imagined it came from their crossing the border, and I pictured them doing the backstroke across the Gulf, but of course they come by land, arriving as haggard and thirsty as the land they come to clear, and now I believe the term comes from the mean work they do, burning and clearing cedar in the heat of the spring days, that soaks their shirts with sweat.

"What do you do first?" I ask.

"The walk around," he says. "Flaps, fuel mixture—"

"Use your checklist." Try as I might to confound him, he is a conscientious student. He walks the airplane's circumference, pulling the chunks of yellow foam from the engine intake, kicking the wheel hubs. I found a rattler sleeping in there once and had to coax it out with a stick.

"Hey, Mister Rattler," I said, "this ain't the Holiday Inn."

Every time I walk around the airplane, especially if I'm alone, I feel as though Jago is with me, watching and judging. I hope he is impressed, and I feel sheepish when I make a mistake. If something funny or exciting happens, as with the rattler, I talk to him. Or rather, I talk and I hope he hears me.

I heard some months ago from an old AWACS pilot now with the airlines that Jago was flying with a NATO unit in Germany and had gotten divorced. My heart leapt when I heard it. I confess, I thought about trying to find him. I still do. I resolve to do it whenever I feel like the past can be overcome. Sometimes I even pick up the phone.

Sometimes I get the urge to tell Dexter about the affair when we are out here toying with the kind of life that used to be Jago's and mine. With Jago, I have known a sort of symphony of flight, in which the mind moves two steps ahead of the hands and in concert with the other pilot. With Dexter, I've had to begin from scratch. This is an aileron. This is a rudder. I'm afraid I'll always be confined to the basic keys and chords, that with Dexter I will never achieve an airplane's operatic heights. And so I want to tell him in order to reclaim what is mine.

I touch him on the shoulder. "Dexter," I say.

And what would happen next? Would I take the advantage, issuing broad, condemning declarations about my past, cursing my miserable fate? *You see! You see!* Or am I Annie the Confessor, contrite and self-loathing, begging for another chance? There's a sense of showmanship here, a stage wanting to be populated. Dexter says I'm too dramatic, that the world is not out to get me (a comment I particularly hate—I never *said* the world was out to get me). I'm tempted to prove him wrong, that my sense of drama is justified.

He's looking at me, afraid he's forgotten some crucial step.

"Good luck," I say, kissing him. "Fly with your head, first, and then your hands."

He fastens the window and begins to taxi along the short parallel to the runway, the grass bowing on either side of him. It's midmorning now and the sun is just beginning its slow deliberate burn on the day. The heat in Saudi smelled acrid with the smoke of oil refineries, but here it smells spicy, like chilies. Dexter stops short of the active and does the final preflight. The airplane is warm and eager to fly. It bounces and skitters under him. He straightens the nose, and it is a pleasure to watch the airplane dart along the runway and open its throat to the sky. Then he is up and over the grassland and the clumps of trees, and now he knows the joy of piloting, watching the land fall away, its geometric patterns spiraling and shifting under the yoke.

The towns here are named with a sense of substance: Art, Junction, Telegraph, Grit. We live in Bresche, pronounced *Brechie*, which is German for gap, named for a crack in the earth near an offshoot of the Guadalupe River. There is a Czech bakery in town that sells *kolaches* and *boukta*, specialties that Dexter calls Tex-Czechs. The first time we flew together, he was amazed by the geography of towns, how they can all exist in your vision at once, as well as the quiet, unfamiliar land between them. Distance and direction are not rigid in an airplane, and even time gives up an element of exactness, so destiny seems not only plausible but also pliant.

What are you thinking, Dex? Are you watching the ground, how it opens under you? Remember to flair. Can you learn to think like me, instinctively, in a world of animate objects, with the past singing canons in your head, *your head, with the past singing canons in your head?*

I stand in the sun and watch him come around in the pattern. I am alone, but Jago is with me, and he says, "I hope he's going through the checklist."

*Gear up. Power. Switches.* Of course there's no gear in a Cessna. I'm a little nervous, but mostly I'm admiring the airplane, its gallant snubbing of gravity. There's something optimistic about small airplane flying, how the motor hums to itself as it lifts into an element it can just barely command.

"He's careful," I say. "He'll make a good pilot."

"You were right to teach him." He wears sunglasses and watches the sky. He is always looking up or to the side so that I only see his face in profile, never head on.

"It's hard," I say. "It's not the same."

Jago says nothing. Even his ghost is too reticent for my taste.

Dexter does a sweep—too low—over the runway and arcs to the left. I should be cross, but I'm astounded, as always, by the dauntlessness of a light plane. When he comes around again, he lines up with the runway and I think he is going to land. I'm standing on the runway, two hundred feet or so from the threshold, and when he flies by I can see his face, calm and concentrating, and then he lifts again, straight out to the south where we go to practice, and is gone.

I walk back to the hangar and sit on the hood of the truck, waiting for the noise of the engine to return, and Jago sits with me. I've cleaned him up. This Jago is better-looking, more poetic, less forgetful. He puts his hand on my arm. He puts his hand right through me and touches my heart.

"Why aren't you here?" I ask. "Why aren't we doing this?"

He doesn't answer, and I continue to goad him, as though by making the right argument strongly enough I will bring him back.

*I am a lion, a stone, a tree.*
*And as the Polar star in me*
*Is fixed my constant heart on thee.*
*Ah, may I stay forever blind.*

It's an old poem and I can't remember the rest. But at the moment the tone, its conviction, is enough.

"Have the wars hardened you?" I ask. "Have they worn you down?"

"It's the same shit," he says.

"At least you're out there."

"Forget it. You're not missing anything."

"Then why do you keep doing it?"

Again, he doesn't answer. Instead, he says, "You should tell him."

"I will."

"You're not hearing me. Tell him soon. Tell him today."

"He'll tell me to stop flying," I say. "I want to fly."

"Tell him."

"If I stop flying, I won't have anything left. Anything *us*."

"Why do you want it so badly, Annie? Why do you want to fly?"

"The same reason you do."

"No, it's not the same. Think about why you want to fly."

"So that I can go where you go."

And then I hear Dexter's engine again. It's loud. I should have heard it minutes ago. He comes around in the pattern with the runway well off to his left, arcs around slowly and lines up straight on the runway.

Good. *Switch the fuel tanks. Gear down. Magnetos.*

There have been stories of crazed lovers who took airplanes and crashed them into their wives' or girlfriends' houses. This won't be one of those stories. I'll never tell Dexter about Jago. This story will fall short of tragedy, and I should count myself lucky.

He's going to land a shade long. It's almost visible how the air sweeps under the wings and cradles them a little longer, holding off the moment of release. I know Dexter feels it, too, that gliding pause before the airplane becomes right with the ground. It's hard to believe, the first time, that you will ever quite feel the ground again, as though it is receding under you, resisting your outstretched wheels. But it lasts no longer than a breath's length, and then the earth is grumbling under you, a shock after all that freedom.

# *Acknowledgments*

NOVEL WRITING IS A SOLITARY PROCESS FLECKED WITH moments of intense collaboration. Legions of thanks to my editors, Dan Conaway and Jill Schwartzman, and my agent, Bill Goodman, for their insight and enthusiasm. I owe beers to Ben Hagar for relating his experience in Somalia. I'm grateful to Mike Butler for our many conversations—his voice remains with me. For their friendship, I thank Cristina Burwell, Dianne Chalifour, and Annette Hendricks. I'm immensely thankful for the time I spent with the Warren Wilson MFA for Writers Program, and particularly with my advisors, Chuck Wachtel, Kai Maristed, Tracy Daugherty, and Tom Paine. My most profound gratitude goes to my husband, Bill, for sharing his experiences in Afghanistan and NATO and especially for his faith and support, without which none of this could have happened.

∽♢∾

*the* ART *of*

UNCONTROLLED

FLIGHT

*a novel*

KIM PONDERS

A Reader's Guide

∽♢∾

The long shadow of a charismatic father led Annie Shaw to decide, as far back as she can remember, to follow in his footsteps and become an Air Force pilot. Years later, after her mother's death and her own graduation from the Academy, Captain A. Shaw is now one of the first female pilots in American history to engage in active combat duty during the first Gulf War. But her pride at earning rank as the only woman in an all-male fraternity offers little solace as the realities of battle change her, forever, into a wary, combat-wise survivor.

## DISCUSSION QUESTIONS

1) The novel both begins and ends with Annie sitting alone, waiting for the arrival of a man (her father in the first chapter and Dexter in the final one). How has Annie changed? How are the men in her life different?

2) Annie has a romantic view of war in the first chapter. Has her perspective changed at the end of the story (see both chapters nine and five)? How?

3) The author switches between first and third point-of-view and between present and past tense. Chapter five is even more fragmented and extends beyond the timeframe of the rest of the novel. Why does the author use this structure? What does it achieve? Does it enhance the novel's themes (war, survival, etc.), or does it distance the reader from the story?

4) How does Annie's guilt about her mother's death feed her character later on? Does it affect the way she makes decisions and interacts with others?

5) In some societies, fire is used as part of a cleansing ritual after battle. What role does fire play in this novel?

**6)** In chapter eight, Annie' father tells her (p. 165): "You needed a hero." Was he right?

**7)** "Uncontrolled Flight" is a technical flying term meaning, as you might imagine, a flight profile (stall, dive, etc.) that the pilot cannot sustain, often preceding a crash. How does "uncontrolled flight" serve as a metaphor in the story?

CPSIA information can be obtained at www.ICGtesting.com
Printed in the USA
LVOW07s2014240915

455526LV00034BB/344/P